Claudia and the Middle School Mystery

THE BABY-SITTERS CLUB
titles in Large-Print Editions:

Claudia and the Middle School Mystery
Ann M. Martin

Gareth Stevens Publishing
MILWAUKEE

For a free color catalog describing Gareth Stevens' list of high-quality books, call 1-800-542-2595 (USA) or 1-800-461-9120 (Canada). Gareth Stevens' Fax: (414) 225-0377.

Library of Congress Cataloging-in-Publication Data

Martin, Ann M., 1955-
    Claudia and the middle school mystery/by Ann M. Martin.
      p. cm. — (The Baby-sitters Club; #40)
      Summary: Claudia is surprised when her math teacher accuses her of cheating on a test and enlists the rest of the Baby-sitters Club to help her clear her name.
      ISBN 0-8368-1420-7
      [1. Cheating—Fiction. 2. Clubs—Fiction.] I. Title. II. Series: Martin, Ann M., 1955- Baby-sitters Club; #40.
    PZ7.M3567585Cli   1995
    [Fic]—dc20   95-22332

Published by Gareth Stevens, Inc., 1555 North RiverCenter Drive, Suite 201, Milwaukee, Wisconsin 53212 in large print by arrangement with Scholastic Inc., 555 Broadway, New York, New York 10012.

Printed in the United States of America

1 2 3 4 5 6 7 8 9 99 98 97 96 95

The author gratefully acknowledges
Ellen Miles
for her help in
preparing this manuscript.

Claudia and the Middle School Mystery

CHAPTER 1

"So, if Gertrude used two thirds of a cup of chocolate to make eight cookies, how much chocolate would be in each cookie?" Janine asked.

I frowned. I bit my lip. I tapped my pencil against my front teeth. "Each cookie would have . . ." Right then I *hated* Gertrude, whoever she was. Why did she have to make cookies, anyway? And why did she have to measure out the chocolate? I'd just dump in as much as I had. I *love* chocolate. And I hate the name Gertrude.

Janine nodded at me encouragingly, smiling as if I'd already come up with the right answer.

I looked up at the picture hanging over my desk. Mimi, as a twelve-year-old, gave me her gentle smile. I looked down at the problem one more time. "It's got to be one twelfth." I said. "One twelfth of a cup in each?" Janine was grinning at me.

"You've got it, Claud!" she said. "I really think you understand it this time." She smiled some more. "Excellent!"

So now you know how much chocolate Gertrude put in each cookie, and so do I, I guess — at least this time. But you don't know who I am, or who Janine might be, or even who Mimi in the picture is.

I'm Claudia Kishi. I'm thirteen and I'm in eighth grade at Stoneybrook Middle School. I have long black hair and almond-shaped eyes (I'm Japanese-American) and in case you haven't already figured it out, I'm not what you would call a scholar. In fact, the test I was studying for was in *remedial* math. That's right. I can't seem to keep up with the rest of my class, at least in certain subjects. I try hard, but maybe not hard enough. The fact is, I'm just not too crazy about things like math and science.

What *am* I crazy about? I'll tell you. First on my list is art. I love drawing, painting, sculpting, making things out of papier-mâché, making collages, making jewelry . . . well, you get the picture.

Next, I love my family. We're pretty close.

2

There's just Mom and Dad and Janine and me. My dad's an investment banker, my mom's a librarian, and my sister, Janine, is a genius. I mean it! She's a junior at Stoneybrook High, but she's taking college courses already. It's, well, it's *interesting* to have a genius in the family. More about Janine later.

Mimi, the one in the picture, was my grandmother. (Of course she wasn't my grandmother yet when that picture was taken.) She died not long ago, but I love that photo of her as a young girl. She looked a lot like me way back then.

I miss Mimi all the time. How can I explain how wonderful she was? Always calm, always gentle — that was Mimi. She understood me better than anyone else ever has. Sometimes I just can't believe that I'll really never see her again. But she'll always be in my heart, and just thinking of her and looking at her picture can make me feel close to her.

Now, where was I? Oh, right. Things that I'm crazy about. Well, I love to baby-sit — so much so that I belong to a club called the Baby-sitters Club — but more about that later, too. I also love to read Nancy Drew mysteries, and I adore junk food. Doritos, M&M's, Twinkies — I never say no to any of it.

My parents, however, don't like me to read Nancy Drew books (they would prefer that I read "classics") and they *really* don't like me to eat junk food. "Proper nutrition is *important* . . ." You know the line.)

So I've learned to hide my secret vices. The Nancy Drew books get stuck under my mattress, or on the top shelf of my closet, or underneath a pile of dirty clothes. The junk food gets stashed anywhere and everywhere — it's always turning up where I least expect it. Last night, for example, when I was looking for my favorite watercolor set, I found a box of Milk Duds that I had hidden about three months ago. (They were still good.)

On this night, though, I wasn't eating any junk food or reading any Nancy Drew books. I was studying for a big test, a huge test, a *killer* test. This math test was going to count for a big part of my final grade. I just *had* to do well on it.

Janine was helping me study. It's kind of a rule in my family (my parents' idea) that somebody has to help me with my homework every night. Mimi used to be my favorite helper of all. She never got impatient with me, she never made me feel dumb, and even though she didn't often tell me so, I always knew that she was very, very proud of whatever I did.

Janine is a different story.

It's not that she's mean or anything — but I just don't think she has any idea of what school is like for me. See, she *loves* school. She'd go to school eight days a week if she could. I don't think she's ever gotten any grade lower than an A–. And you should see the classes she takes! I don't even understand the *names* of most of them — especially the computer ones.

And here she is, helping me try to understand how Gertrude measures chocolate — and why. She must think I'm so dumb. I know it's really nice of her to help me, but I sure wish I didn't need her — or anyone's — help.

I looked back at my math book. All those fractions were kind of making me dizzy. Janine was being unusually patient. She knew this test was important to me.

"So how do you like Mr. Zorzi, Claudia?" she asked. Mr. Zorzi is my math teacher — at least he is for now. See, my regular teacher is out for a few weeks, recovering from an operation, so we have Mr. Zorzi as a long-term substitute.

"He's okay, I guess. I've had him before. He knows it takes me awhile to catch on to

5

some of this stuff," I said, nodding toward my messy notebook.

Frankly, I never think too much about my teachers and whether I like them or not. I just do my best to get through most of my classes without making a total fool of myself. Janine, however, just *loves* some of her teachers — and all of them think that she's the greatest.

Sometimes I get so tired of teachers asking me, "Claudia *Kishi?* Are you Janine's sister? Well, I know I can expect some wonderful work from you, if you're anything like Janine." Of course, they're always disappointed. Except my art teachers. Art is the one thing that I can do well, and Janine has no interest in.

"Okay, Claud. Let's try another one," Janine said. I tried to focus on the numbers in my math book. I was getting tired. "Now, look," she said. "This is an improper fraction. But all we need to do is simplify, then multiply by the reciprocal . . ."

I blanked out for a minute. When Janine got that schoolteacher-ish tone in her voice, she could be hard to listen to. Besides, most of what she was saying sounded like gibberish to me. I know it wasn't right, when she was being nice enough to take the time to help me study — but I just drifted off. I was thinking about this collage I'm working on, and wondering if there would be any good pictures in the new gardening magazine that my mom had brought home that day.

". . . and, by using cross-simplification we find that the train was actually traveling at forty-eight miles per hour, which is . . . Hey Claudia!" Janine snapped her fingers in front of my face. "Earth to Claudia, Earth to Claudia," she said. "Can you read me?"

"Oh, sorry, Janine," I said. "I was just — "

"You were daydreaming again," she said. "I know that look on your face." She frowned and pushed her glasses up — they'd slid down her nose while she was lecturing. "What were you thinking about?"

"Oh, nothing, really," I said. "Let's keep going. What about Problem Five?"

There was no way I was going to tell Janine what I'd been thinking about. I had finished planning my collage, and I'd started to ponder the very deep and important issue of . . . what I was going to wear to school the next day! If Janine only knew.

Janine cares nothing about clothes — and that's just one more thing that makes us very different. Janine would be happy wearing the same white blouse, plaid skirt, red cardigan, and flat shoes every day.

On the other hand, I am of the belief that "you are what you wear." (I'd rather think that than "you are what you eat." If that were true I'd be a Snickers bar or something.) Anyway, I love to dress in a way that some people here in Stoneybrook might call outrageous. For example, here's what I was thinking of wearing the next day: Since I had the big test, I thought I'd start with my lucky earrings — the ones that look like Princess Di's. They're huge (pretend) emeralds, surrounded by thousands of tiny (phony) diamonds. Then I thought I'd work downward from there, wearing my new green-and-blue-tie-dyed T-shirt dress (the casualness of the dress would be an interesting contrast to those fancy earrings) over green leggings.

The only thing I hadn't figured out was the shoes — should I go with my old ballet flats, or the black leather high-tops I'd just gotten? I was having a hard time deciding.

But I wasn't about to ask Janine for her advice. If she had *any* idea of what I'd been thinking about — oh, my lord, I don't even want to imagine what she might say.

So I distracted her by showing off my mathematical brilliance. "Check out Problem Five, Janine," I said again. It was a word problem, about Jack and Jill renting a rowboat and how much it would cost them if they rowed for two and a half hours. (Why I should care, I don't know — you wouldn't catch *me* out in some leaky old rowboat for even five minutes.) I did some quick calculations and a bit of plain old guessing. "The answer would be . . . let's see . . . four dollars and twenty-five cents, right?"

Janine looked at the problem for about two seconds, then beamed at me. "You really do understand, don't you, Claudia? I can see that you're not going to have any problems with this test."

"Right," I said. "No problems at all." I only wish I could have been as sure about it as she was.

CHAPTER 2

When we'd finished going over all the problems, Janine gave me a few quick tips on test-taking in general. I have to admit that by then I was getting kind of tired of all this. But I nodded in all the right places, and soon Janine finished her little speech, wished me good luck on the test, and left my room.

"Thanks a lot, Janine!" I yelled after her. As soon as she was gone I turned on my radio. I hate studying when it's totally quiet, but Janine won't tolerate the radio when she's helping me. Then I turned my attention back to my desk. Time to straighten it up and then finish off the rest of my homework. I gave my math book one more quick glance and then stuck it into my backpack, along with my notebook.

The rest of my homework was a breeze, compared to studying for that test. I raced through it. Then I put down my pencil, got up and stretched, and threw myself onto my bed. "Aaaahh!" I sighed. "All done." I rolled over and reached for the phone.

"Hi, Stace — it's Claud," I said, when my best friend, Stacey McGill, answered the phone at her house. I told Stacey all about my big math test, and about how incredibly nervous I was about it. She tried to calm me down. (She's great in math, just like Janine. She never gets nervous about tests.)

"C'mon, Claud," she said. "What about all that time we've spent going over that stuff?"

It was true. Stacey had been helping me with my math all year, during study halls and sometimes even — when I was especially confused — during lunch.

"I know, Stace, but — "

"But nothing," she interrupted. "You know that material backwards and forwards. You're going to do a great job on that test. I guarantee it!"

This made me feel better, but I still wasn't convinced. I dropped the subject, and we talked for awhile longer, about clothes, about a movie we'd seen, and about our club — the Baby-sitters Club.

"Just think, Claud," she said. "By the time

we have our next meeting you'll have taken the test. It will all be over with."

She was right. We had a club meeting the next day after school. When we'd said good-bye and hung up, I thought about how lucky I was to have such a good friend. And even though Stacey's my *best* friend, I'm especially lucky because I've got a whole gang of other friends, too — the other members of our club.

Maybe I should tell you about them.

First off, there's Kristy Thomas. She's the president — and the founder — of the Baby-sitters Club. Kristy used to live on my street, and I've known her since I was about six months old, probably. Now she lives way across town with her "new" family.

Kristy's *original* family was pretty average — a mom, a dad, two big brothers (Sam and Charlie) and one little one (David Michael). But when David Michael was a baby (he's seven now), Kristy's dad just up and left. I'm not even sure where he lives now — California, maybe? — but Kristy has almost nothing to do with him.

Kristy's mom is a pretty strong woman — I think Kristy takes after her in that way — and she held her family together for years. But then she was lucky enough to fall in love and get married again. And she didn't marry just any old guy. She married Watson Brewer, one of Stoneybrook's millionaires. After that, Kristy and her family moved across town into Watson's mansion (yes, it really *is* a mansion), but of course Kristy remained president of our club.

So these days Kristy's family is anything but average. Besides being a millionaire, Watson is the father of two children from his first marriage — Karen, who's seven, and Andrew, who's four. They're at Watson's every other weekend. But even when they're not there, the house is pretty full.

Who else lives there? Well, there's Emily Michelle, the most adorable baby in the world. She's a two-year-old Vietnamese girl whom Kristy's mom and Watson adopted not long ago. Soon after Emily Michelle came, Nannie moved in, too. Nannie is Kristy's mother's mother, and she watches Emily when nobody else is home.

And as if that weren't enough, there's Boo-Boo and Shannon, too. No, they're not kids — they're pets. Boo-Boo is a mean, fat, old cat. (Watson would probably be mad if he heard me say that, but it's true!) And Shannon is a puppy who's going to turn into a gigantic dog some day — a Bernese Mountain dog, to be exact.

So Kristy's got a busy life at home. But I think she likes it that way. She's always doing two or three things at once and planning a fourth at the same time. She's a whirlwind with great ideas (like the one about starting our club). She's so busy that she doesn't care much about her looks — which, in fact, there's nothing wrong with. Kristy has brown hair and eyes, and a really friendly, open face. She's pretty, but she doesn't seem to want to bother with clothes, or makeup, or hairdos, or any of that. She wears the same thing every day — running shoes, jeans, a turtleneck, and maybe a sweater, if it's cold. I guess you'd have to call her a tomboy.

Kristy's only fault may be that she kind of has a big mouth. At times things just slip out of her mouth — but usually it's not a problem with the rest of us. We're used to it.

Even Mary Anne Spier isn't bothered by the blunt way Kristy can talk. And that's saying something, because Mary Anne is the most sensitive soul in the universe. Who's Mary Anne? She's the secretary of our club, and Kristy's best friend, which is kind of funny if you think about it — they're so different. Mary

Anne is as quiet as Kristy is loud, and as shy as Kristy is outgoing.

They do look alike, though. Mary Anne's a little taller than Kristy (Kristy's the shortest person in our class), but her hair and eyes are the same shade of brown as Kristy's.

However, Mary Anne's clothes are trendier than Kristy's, she's less of a talker (she's a great listener, in fact), and she's more of a romantic. Maybe that's why she's the only one in our club who has a steady boyfriend. His name is Logan Bruno, he's incredibly cute, and he's *in* our club, believe it or not. (He's just an associate member, but I'll explain all about that later.)

Sometimes it still amazes me that Mary Anne is *allowed* to have a boyfriend. I still think of her father as strict, even though he's actually eased up a lot recently. See, Mary Anne's father raised her on his own — her mother died when Mary Anne was just a tiny baby — and I guess he thought that being very strict was best. But he got married again not too long ago, and that seems to have softened him up a bit. Actually, he was beginning to be less strict even before that — back when he was just dating his future wife.

And who *is* that wife? I thought you'd never

15

ask. Mr. Spier just happens to be married to the mother of another member of our club, Dawn Schafer. How did they meet? It's a crazy story. Mrs. Schafer and Mr. Spier were high-school sweethearts, right here in Stoneybrook. But Mrs. Schafer left town for California, and that's where she met and married Dawn's father. They had Dawn and her younger brother, Jeff, but later they got divorced. Then Mrs. Schafer and Dawn and Jeff moved back to Stoneybrook, and it wasn't long before the high-school romance bloomed all over again! Isn't that great?

So now Mary Anne and Dawn are stepsisters — and also best friends. (Yes, Mary Anne has *two* best friends.) Mary Anne and her father and Tigger (that's Mary Anne's kitten) moved into Dawn's mother's house because it was bigger. Now they all live there happily, except for Jeff, who missed California and his father so much that he moved back there. Dawn misses them terribly, but she tries to visit the California part of her family whenever she can.

You'd know Dawn for a California girl the minute you saw her. She's absolutely gorgeous. Blonde? They don't come any blonder. Her clothes are great — casual, fun, and stylish. She loves health food and the sun, and she's just basically what I'd have to call "mellow." She knows her own mind — for example, she doesn't get tempted by all the great junk food I always have.

One thing that *does* tempt Dawn is a mystery. And she also loves ghost stories. Her favorite ghost story, in fact, is the one about her own house! That's right — her house may be haunted. There's this secret passage in that old farmhouse, and someday I'm sure Dawn will catch the ghost that she believes lives there.

I don't think Stacey believes in the ghost. (That's Stacey McGill, my best friend.) She's blonde, and pretty, and very smart. Stacey grew up in New York City! But now she lives in Stoneybrook, with her mom. She and I became friends when she first moved here — probably because we both have sophisticated taste in clothes — but now our friendship is much deeper. I was *crushed* when she moved back to the city (her dad's company transferred him) but it wasn't long before she'd moved back here again. Of course I was thrilled, even if the *reason* for her move wasn't the greatest — it was because her parents had gotten divorced.

Stacey's handling the divorce well — she visits her dad in the city as often as she can. And she and her mom are close.

Mr. and Mrs. McGill used to be kind of overprotective of Stacey, because Stacey has diabetes. That means that she has to be very careful about what she eats and when she eats it, or else her blood sugar gets all out of whack and she can get extremely sick. It all has something to do with her pancreas, but the complete scientific story behind it is more than I can remember. (I almost failed biology.)

Stacey takes good care of herself, checking her own blood sugar and giving herself injections (ew) of insulin. She tries not to let the diabetes cramp her style, but lately I've noticed that she seems kind of tired and weak all the time. I hope she's okay.

The last but not least of my baby-sitting friends are Mallory Pike and Jessica (everyone calls her Jessi) Ramsey. They're younger than the rest of us (they're in sixth grade) but they're pretty cool. They're best friends, and like most best friends they're different in some ways and alike in others.

This is how they're alike: They both love to read (especially horse stories), they both wish their parents would stop treating them like

18

babies (eleven is a hard age), and they both come from close families.

This is how they're different: Mallory's family is *huge* — she has seven younger brothers and sisters. Jessi's family is smaller — just a little sister, Becca, and a baby brother, nicknamed Squirt — and also, they're black, while Mal and her family are white. Of course, Jessi's color makes no difference to any of us, but there were plenty of people in Stoneybrook who felt otherwise, at least at first. Now I'd say that Jessi is pretty happily settled here. Another difference: Mallory loves to write and draw (she hopes to be a children's book author and illustrator someday) while Jessi's passion is ballet (she's a *really* good dancer and practices all the time).

So those are my friends. I'm pretty lucky to have every one of them. But I knew that the next day, during math class, it would be just me against good old Gertrude. I would be on my own.

CHAPTER 3

"Okay, people," said Mr. Zorzi, trying to be heard over the roar of everyone talking at once. "Let's get ready for this test." He stood at the front of the room with a stack of papers in his hands. "Books on the floor beside your desks."

Then he walked along the front row of desks, giving each kid a bunch of papers. "Pass them back, please." He folded his arms and watched as the tests were distributed. "This test will count for a large portion of your grade. But don't worry — I think all of you know the material. I'm sure you'll do well."

I looked down at the paper that had landed on my desk, and gulped. There were a lot of problems on it. Fractions and decimals were scattered like land mines all over the page.

I glanced up at Mr. Zorzi. He saw me looking up and gave me a little smile. Then he pointed at the clock. I got the message — time to get started.

I focused on the first problem. It didn't seem to make any sense. I blinked and looked again. It still looked like nothing but a jumble of words and numbers. Oh, no! All of a sudden I felt dizzy. What was I going to do? There was no way I was going to make it through this test if I couldn't even make sense of the first problem.

Then I remembered something Janine had told me. "If you get nervous, Claudia, just take a few deep breaths." I did that. Now, what else had she said? I thought for a minute. Then I heard Janine's voice in my mind. "Remember, Claudia — you don't have to do the test in any special order. If the first question looks too hard, find one that you *can* do, and then you can always go back."

I looked down the page. There! Problem Six! I was sure I knew how to do that one. It only took a couple of minutes, and by the time I finished it, all the stuff I'd studied had come back to me. I went back up to Problem One and worked straight through the rest of the test.

I didn't work fast — I took my time and made sure not to make any "foolish mistakes," as Mr. Zorzi calls them, like doing the whole problem right but then adding two and three and getting six.

When the bell rang, I nearly jumped out of my seat. I'd been concentrating so hard! I glanced over the problems one more time and then handed in my test. As I walked out of the room, I was grinning. I must have looked like a jerk, but I just felt so good. I had never felt that way after taking a test before. I *knew* I had done a good job. I was sure I'd get at least a B on the test — maybe even an A!

The rest of the day dragged a little, probably because I couldn't wait for it to be over. I was really looking forward to our club meeting that afternoon. I couldn't wait to tell Stacey and the others about how well I'd done on the test.

When I got home, I tried to work on my collage, but I felt too excited. By 5:15, it seemed like I'd been waiting forever for the meeting to start. I'd cleaned up my room a little and put out some snacks — M&M's and Fritos for me, Kristy, Mary Anne, Jessi, and Mallory, and whole-wheat crackers for Dawn and Stacey.

Finally I heard someone pounding up the stairs. (Nobody knocks on the front door or rings the bell when they come to meetings —

they just let themselves in.) It was Kristy. Being president, she feels it's important to be on time. She's almost always the first to arrive.

She sat down in the director's chair by my desk, put on her visor, and tucked a pencil behind her ear. She was ready for the meeting. "How's it going, Claud?" she asked.

I started to tell her about my test, but then I thought maybe I should wait until the others were here so I wouldn't have to tell everything twice.

I looked at Kristy in her chair and thought about all the other times I'd seen her sitting there. The Baby-sitters Club had been going strong for a long time, I realized. I thought back to how it had all begun.

Kristy got the idea for the club back in the beginning of seventh grade. One night her mom was trying to get an after-school sitter for David Michael (Kristy's little brother, remember?), which wasn't usually a problem, since most of the time either Kristy or Sam or Charlie would be able to sit for him. But anyway, that time, none of them could. And Mrs. Thomas (she wasn't married to Watson yet) could not find a sitter, no matter how many phone calls she made. Kristy started thinking. Wouldn't it be a great service to parents if they could reach a whole bunch of sitters with just one phone call?

And that's why we meet in my room every Monday, Wednesday, and Friday from 5:30 to 6:00. Why my room? Because I'm the only one of us with my own phone. (I think that's why I got to be vice-president, too!) We couldn't tie up our parents' phones for all those times. During that half hour, parents call and arrange for our services. (They get our names from other parents, or from the fliers we send out.) It's as simple as that.

Well, it's not *quite* that simple. It takes a lot of figuring out to know which of us is available for which jobs, and that's where Mary Anne comes in, as our secretary. She knows all our schedules — my art classes, Jessi's dance classes, Mallory's orthodonist appointments — all of that. And she keeps track of it in the club record book. (The record book was Kristy's idea, too — she's into "official" stuff — and I must admit that it helps things run smoothly.) I don't know how Mary Anne does it, to tell you the truth. She's never made a mistake!

The record book doesn't only have appointments in it. It also has all kinds of vital information like our clients' addresses and phone numbers, *plus* detailed records on which kids have which allergies and which ones only eat peanut butter and bananas — stuff like that.

We also keep track of how much money we make, but that's Stacey's job. She's the club treasurer, mainly because she's such a math whiz. It's lucky that she's not as sensitive as Mary Anne, because if she were, she might have a hard time with the worst part of her job: collecting dues. We all hate paying up, and when Monday (dues day) rolls around, we always whine and complain for a few minutes before parting with our money.

We always do pay up, though, because the dues are important. What do we use the money for? Well, club stuff. Like paying Kristy's brother Charlie to drive Kristy back and forth to BSC meetings — she lives too far away to walk or ride her bike like the rest of us. And for fun things, like pizza parties or food for club sleepovers.

We also use some of the money for our Kid-Kits, which are really just boxes that we've decorated so that they look pretty cool, then filled with all kinds of goodies for kids to play with. Books, toys, stickers, crayons — nothing fancy, but fun things that help to distract kids on a rainy day. Guess who had the idea for Kid-Kits. Kristy, of course.

Anyway, Stacey does a great job of keeping track of our treasury. She also records how much we've earned on our jobs, though *that* money is ours to keep. It's just interesting to know how much we make overall.

You might be wondering what Dawn's job is in the club. Well, she's the alternate officer. That means if anyone else is sick or can't make it to a meeting, she fills in. She was treasurer for awhile when Stacey had moved back to New York. And I think she's done everybody else's job at least once.

Mallory and Jessi don't really have jobs, since they are junior officers. "Junior officer" means that they are not allowed to sit at night (except for their own brothers and sisters). But they get plenty of work in the afternoons, and that helps free the rest of us up for nighttime sitting jobs.

I've already told you a little about one of our associate members, Logan. We have another, Shannon Kilbourne, who lives in Kristy's neighborhood. The associate members don't come to regular meetings or sit on a regular basis, but they've bailed us out of a tough spot more than once. It's rare that none of us can make time for a sitting job, but it does happen, and when it does, we're happy to have Shannon and Logan to call on.

There's one last thing I haven't told you about yet — maybe because it's my least favorite thing about the BSC. That's the club notebook. (Not the record book — this is different.) The club notebook is where we each have to write up every job that we've had — who we sat for, what happened, etc. Not only do we have to write in it, but we also have to *read* it every week, so we know what went on when our friends were baby-sitting.

I won't even tell you whose idea the notebook was — I'm sure you've guessed. I don't mean to complain about it — it's actually a really good idea and it does help keep us informed about things. But it seems like a lot of work. And sometimes, I admit it, I'm a little embarrassed by how bad my spelling is. My friends never laugh at me, but I can guess what they must be thinking.

It's kind of incredible to think back to the beginnings of the club and then look at it now. It's really a successful business! We're all such different people, yet somehow all of us have pooled our talents and the club is the result.

Anyway, back to the meeting. Kristy cleared her throat loudly. I looked up and saw that, while I'd been lost in my thoughts, everyone else had drifted in. The meeting was about to start.

I met Stacey's eyes as Kristy called the meeting to order. I smiled and gave her the thumbs-up sign. She raised her eyebrows and then tilted her head and smiled, as if to say, "See? I told you you'd do fine." Stacey and I have been close for so long now that we don't always need words to talk.

No sooner had Kristy started the meeting than the phone began to ring. Calls were coming in a mile a minute — everybody in Stoneybrook seemed to need a sitter that week. I was dying to tell my friends about the test, but it had to wait.

Finally, the calls slowed down. The meeting was almost over. The snacks I'd put out were all gone, so I rustled around in my favorite hiding places (like my hollowed-out book) and turned up some Oreos.

"Time to celebrate!" I said. I told them about the test, and how I'd gotten so nervous at first. Then I told them how I ended up breezing through all the problems.

"Congratulations, Claud!" said Kristy. Stacey just looked at me with a big smile. Mary Anne was more cautious.

"Don't you think you should wait to celebrate until you get your test back?" she asked.

She was right, I knew it. But I'd know my
grade the next day. And the exact grade I got
didn't really matter, anyway. I just *knew* I'd
done well. And it felt terrific.

CHAPTER 4

"As I promised, I have your tests graded and ready to return to you," said Mr. Zorzi at the beginning of math class the next day. "But I'm going to pass them out a little later in the period. We're starting on Chapter Twelve today, and we'll need to concentrate on the material."

Oh, no! I couldn't believe I was going to have to make it through half the period without knowing my grade. How nerve-racking. I felt like I was going to explode if I didn't know soon. I was still sure I'd done well, but Mary Anne's comment had echoed in my mind all night. I knew she hadn't meant to upset me — and what she'd said was only common sense — but I just wouldn't feel at ease until I'd seen my grade.

Mr. Zorzi had held back on returning our tests so that we would pay attention to the new material, but his plan sure did backfire when it came to me. I don't have a clue about what he taught us for the rest of the class.

Finally (it seemed like *hours* later), Mr. Zorzi finished telling us about ratios and proportions. My nails were bitten down as far as they could go. Mr. Zorzi *strolled* to his desk (In my mind I was saying, "Come *on*, come *on!*"), picked up the pile of papers, and smiled at the class.

"With a few exceptions, I'm very proud of your performance on this test," he said. Then he passed out our tests.

"Put mine upside down, Mr. Zorzi," called the kid next to me. "I don't want anybody to see my grade." About three other boys said the same thing. But I knew they weren't really as worried as they sounded. And of course, as soon as they got their papers back, they held them up and showed them to everybody.

The paper landed on my desk upside down. Closing my eyes and taking a deep breath, I turned it over. I opened my eyes. There was my grade, written in red ink at the top of the sheet. Ninety-four percent. An A–! I almost shouted out loud. I was so happy and so relieved. It hadn't all been in my mind — I really *had* done well.

"Let's go over the test quickly," said Mr. Zorzi. "I want you all to look at Problem Three. Who got that right?"

Almost everybody raised their hands. "How did you figure that out, Heather?" asked Mr. Zorzi. She answered, but I wasn't really listening. I just kept looking at that beautiful A– for the rest of the period.

Mr. Zorzi worked quickly through the whole test. Finally, the bell rang, and everyone got up to leave. As I was gathering my books together, I heard Mr. Zorzi speaking loudly over the noise we were all making. "Shawna Riverson and Claudia Kishi," he said, "please stop at my desk on your way out."

I figured that he must want to congratulate me on my especially high grade, and to tell me how proud he was that I studied so hard for the test. I couldn't really guess why he wanted to talk to Shawna. After all, she almost always gets good grades. She's one of the best students in the class.

I walked up to Mr. Zorzi's desk with a big smile on my face. Shawna was right beside me, looking bewildered. Mr. Zorzi didn't return my smile. I stood there next to Shawna, waiting for Mr. Zorzi to speak. He looked very stern.

"I'd like both of you to take out your test papers," he said. I didn't have to look far — I hadn't even put mine away. I had been planning to show it off to Stacey and the others. Shawna pulled hers out of a notebook.

"Put them side by side," said Mr. Zorzi, "and tell me if you notice something." I saw it right away. We'd both gotten the exact same grade — ninety-four percent. I said so to Mr. Zorzi.

"That's right, Claudia," he said, still sounding pretty grim. "But there's something else." He pointed at my paper. "See Problem Five?" I looked where he was pointing. I'd gotten that one wrong.

"I think I understand what I did there, Mr. Zorzi," I said. "I should have multiplied by the reciprocal instead of dividing, right?" Beside me, Shawna nodded as if she agreed.

"That's not the point, Claudia," he said. "Look at Shawna's paper." I did. And I realized something. She'd gotten the same question wrong — in the exact same way.

Mr. Zorzi went over our tests with us. We'd each only gotten three problems wrong, but we'd each done them wrong in the same way. I still didn't understand what Mr. Zorzi was getting at, though. Maybe he thought we

33

should be tutored together or something.

"Girls," he said, "the probability of this happening is almost zero." He looked at each of us in turn. "Do you realize what this suggests to me?"

I turned to Shawna. For just a second, I saw something like fear in her eyes. Confused, I looked back at Mr. Zorzi.

"One of you must have copied from the other," he said. He was looking straight at me.

Did you ever hear the expression "my blood ran cold?" Well, that's what happened to me. The second he said that, I felt like there were icicles in my veins. I shivered. Then, just as suddenly, I felt hot all over, and I knew my face must have turned bright red. I just couldn't believe what Mr. Zorzi was saying.

Shawna spoke up right away. "Mr. Zorzi, you're not my regular teacher, so you don't know me that well." I turned to look at her, feeling like I was in the middle of a dream. Shawna went on. "If you did, you'd know that I would never cheat on a test." She sounded so sure of herself.

Mr. Zorzi looked closely at her and then nodded. "You can go, Shawna," he said. She gathered her books together and left the room without looking at me.

I stood with my head down, trying to understand what was happening. I felt like a complete jerk. Why couldn't I have spoken up like Shawna did? Of course, I knew right away that she *must* have copied my paper. I knew for sure that I hadn't cheated. But there was no way that Mr. Zorzi — or any teacher, for that matter — would take my word against hers.

Shawna is a really good student — in everything but math. But even in our remedial math class, she usually gets the best grades. She always studies hard for tests. Shawna is also incredibly popular. She has this huge group of friends, she's in the Drama Club (and always gets the leading roles in their plays), and she's a member of the Pep Squad. Miss Stoneybrook Middle School, that's Shawna.

And who was I? Good old Claudia "C-student" Kishi. Of course Mr. Zorzi assumed I was the one who had cheated. Why shouldn't he? I stopped myself. Wait a minute. He shouldn't! So I wasn't the best student in the history of the world. I was honest, at least. I'd never even *thought* of cheating on a test!

"Mr. Zorzi," I said. "I know this doesn't look good. But there must be some explanation! There's no way I would ever — "

But Mr. Zorzi interrupted me. "Claudia," he said gently, "I've seen your record, and I know you must be tired of having to work so hard in order to get passing grades in your classes." He took off his glasses and rubbed his eyes. "But looking at somebody else's paper isn't the answer."

"But Mr. Zorzi," I said. "I didn't — "

He held up his hand. "I'm sorry, Claudia, but I'm going to have to talk to the principal about this." He frowned. "Cheating is serious business."

As if I didn't know.

Mr. Zorzi went on. "And he'll probably want to let your regular math teacher know, just so that everyone can be aware of the incident."

I nodded miserably. I felt like a shipwreck victim, drifting away on a tiny rubber raft, helpless to do anything but watch as the ship tilted and then — *whooosh!* — went down.

But Mr. Zorzi wasn't finished. "And, of course, the principal will be calling your parents."

The tiny rubber raft sprang a leak and sank. It was all over. I couldn't even begin to think about how my parents would react to a phone call like that.

Suddenly I felt very, very tired. I could see that there was no point in trying to say anything else to Mr. Zorzi. He had his mind made up. He wasn't being mean about it or anything — I think just about any teacher would have acted the same way, dismissing Shawna and putting the blame on me. After all, why would Shawna cheat? She wasn't the one who got C's in all her subjects.

"Claudia?" Mr. Zorzi asked softly. I looked up. I'd been lost in a fog for a minute. "You can go now," he said.

I gathered my books to my chest. Then I glanced at my math test, lying there on the desk. Obviously, I wasn't supposed to take it with me. Mr. Zorzi needed it for evidence.

I walked out of the room without saying a word. I was in a complete daze. Somehow I found my way to my locker. I leaned against it for a moment with my eyes closed. I didn't feel like crying — I didn't feel anything at all. I was numb.

Finally, I opened my locker and put my math book away. I never wanted to see it again.

I can't really remember much about the rest of the day — only that it was probably the worst one I've ever spent in school. And that includes the day I went back to school a few days after Mimi died, when everyone was afraid to speak to me. That was bad, but this was worse.

I spent my lunch hour in the girls' room, not wanting to see any of my friends. Luckily, I didn't have any classes with Stacey for the rest of the day. She would have taken one look at me and known something was wrong.

I knew I'd call her that night and tell her all about it. After all, she was my best friend. And I could count on her to tell the others, so I wouldn't have to. I knew she'd be nice about it — supportive and all that — but boy, did I wish I didn't have to tell *anyone*. If only it had never happened.

What a day! I felt like I had been on a roller coaster. I'd started off so excited, and here I was at the end of the day, feeling more miserable than I'd ever felt before. All I could think was, If this is what I get for studying, I may never crack a book again.

CHAPTER 5

Tuesday

Excitement at the Pikes' this afternoon. As soon as I got there I could see that it was going to be a day to remember. Everything seemed kind of hectic. Not that it's ever calm at the Pikes! But little did I know what "was about to transpire," as they say in those old-fashioned novels...

Stacey did have a pretty wild time at the Pikes' that afternoon. It was the same day I'd been accused of cheating, but luckily she didn't even know about that yet. She had enough on her hands as it was.

As Stacey said, it's never calm at the Pikes'. I told you that Mallory had a big family, but let me introduce them all just so you get the whole picture.

Mallory's the oldest. She's eleven and kind of quiet (at least in relation to the rest of the Pikes) and . . . well, I've already told you a lot about her. After Mal come the triplets — Byron, Adam, and Jordan. They're ten. And if you think that one ten-year-old boy can be a noisy handful, you should try sitting for three at a time! Actually, Byron's kind of sensitive and a little calmer than the others — but Jordan and Adam make up for it by being extremely wild.

Then, after the triplets, there's Vanessa. She's nine, and she thinks she's Emily Dickinson or something. She wants to be a poet, and she goes around speaking in rhyme half the time. Then there's Nicky, who's eight. He longs to be old enough to play with the triplets, but unfortunately they leave him out of things too often. Most of the time, Nicky ends up hanging around with Margo. She's seven, and she's a pretty good kid. And then, finally, there's Claire, the baby of the family. She's five, and she seems to be in a permanent "silly" phase. She loves to play "pretend," and she generally refers to people as "silly-billy-goo-goo's."

So this is what Stacey saw when she arrived at the Pikes': Mallory was dashing out the door, trying to be on time for a sitting job of her own. She barely had time to say hello to Stacey. Mrs. Pike was trying to round up Margo, Nicky, and Vanessa for a trip to the mall, but no sooner would she have all three of them in the car than one would jump out, claiming to have forgotten something that he or she desperately needed.

"Hi, Stacey," said Mrs. Pike with a sigh. "Thanks for being on time. I know I must be crazy to take all three of them clothes shopping at once, but at least it's better than taking everyone!"

Stacey tried for a moment (she told me later) to picture a trip to the mall with all eight Pikes. The image was too horrible to think about.

She smiled at Mrs. Pike. "Why don't you just stay with the others, and I'll get Vanessa," she said.

She went into the house and found Vanessa in the living room, searching through a huge box of toys, games, and other stuff. "Vanessa," she said, "your mother is waiting for you. Better get going!"

Vanessa looked up. "My green notebook I must find," she said, "for I have a special poem in mind."

"Not now, Vanessa," Stacey said, smiling. "Try to remember it, and you can write it down when you get back." She walked Vanessa out the door and then waved as Mrs. Pike backed down the driveway.

Suddenly, Stacey sensed someone behind her. She turned, and saw *three* someones — the triplets. Each of them was making a different gruesome face. Claire stood nearby, giggling.

"Hey, you guys!" said Stacey. "Nice faces! What if they stay that way?" They laughed, knowing that she was teasing. Then, just as Stacey was about to suggest that they go outside to play since it was such a nice day (and since they seemed a little wound up), Adam announced that they were going to play baseball in the backyard.

"And *you* can't come!" he said to Claire, sticking out his tongue.

"I don't care, Adam-silly-billy-goo-goo," she answered. "Me and Stacey are going to play hopstotch."

"It's *'hopscotch,'* you dummy," said Jordan.

"Jordan," said Stacey. "Be nice!" But she knew he didn't really mean it. "Okay, have fun, guys," she said, waving them into the backyard.

Then she turned to Claire. "Hopscotch?" she asked.

"Can we?" asked Claire. "Please? Margo *never* plays hopstotch with me anymore."

"Sure, Claire," said Stacey. "Let's find some chalk."

They found some pink chalk in the toy box and went out to the driveway to draw the board. Stacey started right in, drawing the first three boxes stacked on top of each other, then a fourth and fifth side-by-side stacked on top of them.

"No, Stacey!" said Claire. "You're not doing it right." She pointed at one of the lines Stacey had drawn, which *was* a little crooked.

Stacey tried to be patient. Claire always needed to have things done "just so," and sometimes it took a long time until she was satisfied. "Okay," said Stacey. "Look, I'll fix that line like this, and then you can fill in the numbers. Can you make a one here and a two here?"

Claire's a pretty smart kid (all the Pikes are) and she knows her numbers really well. She and Stacey worked on the board for quite awhile, Stacey drawing the boxes and Claire filling in the numbers. Finally, it was done.

They couldn't start to play, though — not until Claire had found a special "lucky" stone to toss down, and helped Stacey find just the right one, too. Then she went through an elaborate ritual to decide who got the first turn.

At last, the game began. Stacey threw down her stone and hopped. When she'd finished her turn (of course, she'd pretended to slip so that her turn wouldn't last forever and Claire wouldn't get even more impatient than she already was), Claire threw down *her* stone. She didn't like where it landed, and she tried to get Stacey to let her throw again, but Stacey wouldn't let her. (Mean old Stacey!)

Then, Claire began to hop. Hop, hop . . . *CRASH!* Claire went tumbling over the neatly

drawn squares. Stacey held her breath. Sometimes if you don't make a big deal about a fall,
the kid won't, either. But then Claire began
to bawl.

Stacey ran over to where she lay and took
a look at the knee Claire was pointing to. This
wasn't a false alarm. She'd skinned it pretty
badly. And she'd skinned the other knee,
too — and also one of her hands.

Stacey looked over to where the triplets
were playing ball. They were so absorbed in
their game that they'd barely noticed Claire
crying. "Adam! Jordan! Byron!" Stacey yelled.
"I'm taking Claire inside to clean her up. Don't
go anywhere without telling me first, okay?"
They nodded and kept on tossing the ball
around.

Then Stacey scooped up Claire and took her
inside. She washed out the scrapes as gently
as she could, while Claire gave her careful
directions through her sobs. "Now put on
some thirst-aid cream and then a bandage,"
said Claire. Stacey followed orders, rummaging in the medicine cabinet to find the first-
aid cream.

Claire was so interested in the bandaging
procedure that she'd begun to forget how
much her hand and knees hurt. Her sobbing

had slowed to a sniffle as Stacey applied the last bandage.

Just then, Stacey heard a loud *SMASH* from downstairs. "What — " she said. She realized immediately that the triplets had managed to break something. She ran down the stairs, Claire hobbling after her, and out the door.

There were all three boys crowded around one of the basement windows. Their bat and a pile of gloves lay on the ground, but the ball was nowhere in sight.

Stacey put her hands on her hips. "Okay, which one of the wrecking crew is responsible for this?" she asked. The triplets looked at each other, then looked back at Stacey. All three shrugged in unison.

"What's going on?" asked Stacey. "All I asked was which one of you did it."

The triplets shrugged again. Then Byron spoke up. "It's like this movie we saw," he said. *"The Three Musketeers.* All for one . . ." he started, and then Jordan and Adam joined in, "and one for all!"

"We've decided to be like them. We'll never turn in a fellow triplet again!" said Jordan.

"Yeah!" said Adam. "We're a team."

Stacey rolled her eyes. Then she cleaned up the broken glass. She made Claire and the triplets stand off to the side — she didn't need any more injuries that afternoon.

When Mrs. Pike got home, Stacey had to tell her what had happened. Mrs. Pike rolled her eyes, too, when she heard about the Three Musketeers. Then she questioned the boys herself.

They still wouldn't tell which one of them had broken the window.

"You know, guys," she said, "ordinarily I'd let this go. But this is the *fourth* window you've broken in the last three months. This can't continue." She stopped to think. "Since you won't tell me who did it, I'm going to have to punish all three of you. You'll be grounded until you admit which one of you is the culprit. Also, none of you will get an allowance until that window is paid for."

Stacey was sure that such a tough punishment would convince the triplets to abandon their pact, but they didn't give in. They just looked at each other silently, turned around, and headed for their room. Stacey watched them go, shaking her head. At least, she thought, you never got bored sitting for the Pikes!

CHAPTER 6

And what was *I* doing while Stacey was sitting at the Pikes'? Well, I was sitting, too. In my room, with the door closed. I wasn't doing homework. I wasn't listening to the radio. I wasn't working on my collage. I wasn't even reading Nancy Drew. And I wasn't eating the Cheetos that I'd hidden the day before in my sock drawer. I was just sitting.

I was thinking, too — or at least *trying* to think. I still couldn't get a handle on what had happened in math class that day, and I hadn't figured out what to do about it. I knew I was innocent, but what I didn't know was how to get everybody else to believe me.

I heard Janine come home, but I didn't call out to her. I wasn't ready to talk to anyone about my problem. Luckily, she didn't come upstairs to work on her computer, like she usually does. Instead, she started getting dinner ready in the kitchen. Good! That meant I could just keep on sitting.

A little while later I heard my mom come home. She and Janine were talking when the phone rang. Was this *the* call? Was the principal on the other end, telling my mother what a horrible person I was? I didn't even want to know. I stayed in my room.

Soon I heard my mom and Janine talking again. I couldn't make out what they were saying, but their voices sounded serious. Then my dad came home. I heard his footsteps go into the kitchen. More talking.

What would happen if I just stayed in my room for the rest of my life? I wouldn't go hungry for quite awhile, with all the junk food I had hidden all over the place. And I could entertain myself by reading mysteries and working on art projects. The more I thought about it, the better the idea sounded. I nodded to myself. Yup, staying in my room was definitely the best plan.

"Claudia!" my mom called up the stairs. "Dinner!"

I didn't answer. I folded my arms and stayed where I was.

Five minutes later she called again. "Claudia, honey!" she said. "We're having tacos!"

Sure enough, I could smell the popcorn-y smell of tacos warming in the oven. Tacos are one of my favorite foods. I guess it's because they're about as close to junk food as you can get when you're sitting around the table with your family. Mmm, a big crunchy taco filled with all that delicous spicy beef and then stuffed to the brim with toppings . . .

Once I'd started thinking about tacos, I couldn't stop. Suddenly I decided that staying in my room for the rest of my life might not be such a hot idea after all. "Coming!" I yelled.

I slid into my seat at the table just as Janine brought in a big platter of tacos. On the table were a whole lot of little bowls filled with grated cheese, tomatoes, onions, lettuce, and sour cream. Yum! I took a taco and started to pile on the extras. Everybody else was busy doing the same.

Just as I was about to bite into the *very* stuffed, juicy, dripping mess I had created, my mom spoke up.

"Claudia, honey," she said. "I got a call from your principal this afternoon."

I gulped. Suddenly the taco I was holding didn't look so tempting anymore.

"Do you want to tell us what happened today?" she asked.

I looked down at my hands, which were now folded in my lap. The taco lay forgotten on my plate. I didn't know what to say.

"I — I don't know what to say," I said. "I didn't do it." I swallowed hard. All of a sudden I felt like I was going to start bawling any minute.

"We'd like to believe you, Claud," said my father.

They'd *like* to believe me? Oh, no! Even my parents thought I was a cheater. I bit my lip to keep from crying. Then Janine spoke up.

"I *do* believe her. There's no question about it. Claudia knew that material cold." She was speaking very quickly. "I helped her study, remember?" She glanced at each of my parents in turn. "Besides, Claudia is *not* a cheater."

My parents exchanged a look. Then my mother got up and came around to where I was sitting. "I'm so sorry, honey. Janine's right. I don't know how I could have ever thought — " she said, as she hugged me tight. And I hugged her, working hard to hold in my tears.

"You know," she said, as she walked back

to her seat. "The principal didn't sound all that sure about it, either. He said he was just 'informing' us about the situation. I guess it's all part of the procedure."

"I think we should go to your school and speak to the principal in person. Straighten this whole thing out," said my dad.

That was the last thing I wanted. I just knew that if they got involved, things might become even worse. I had to figure out how to handle this on my own. "No, Dad," I said. "Please. I can take care of it."

"But Claudia," said my mother, "the principal said that Mr. Zorzi is going to have to give you an F on this test. What will that mean for your final grade?"

An F. I couldn't believe it. The one time I'd actually studied hard enough to earn an A–, fair and square — and I was going to end up with an F. "Don't worry, Mom," I said, sounding more sure of myself than I felt. "I'll work it out." Inside, though, *I* was worried. I'd have to get practically straight A's on every other math test from here on, or I really might fail the class.

And I knew that if I failed math, I might be forced to give up one of the most important things in my life — the Baby-sitters Club.

There was no way my parents would continue to let me spend all that time on an "outside" activity if I was failing classes at school.

I picked up my taco and tried to finish it, but it tasted pretty much like sawdust. (Not that I've ever actually *eaten* sawdust, but you know what I mean.) My parents *said* they believed me, but I was getting a strange feeling from them. Were they a little suspicious? Did they have just the tiniest doubt about my honesty? Were they feeling . . . disappointed in me? I could hardly stand it.

Finally, dinner was over. I helped Janine clear the table, and then we cleaned up the kitchen together. We weren't talking much, but I was giving her a lot of grateful looks. It's funny, Janine and I have definitely been through some rough times, but no matter what, she's my big sister. And there are times when that means everything.

When I'd finished wiping the last pot, I headed for my room. I was still feeling very upset, and I needed some time to figure out what to do. Janine followed me upstairs and into my room. I threw myself on the bed.

"Claudia," said Janine, "it'll be all right." She sat down at my desk. "Look, I'll be glad to help you with your math for the rest of the year. If we work really hard, you won't fail the class, even if Mr. Zorzi does give you that F."

"But Janine," I said. "It's so unfair. I got an A– on that test!"

Janine looked shocked. I guess the principal hadn't told anybody what my actual grade had been. Then she gave me a big smile. "Congratulations, Claudia!" she said. "That's fantastic! I knew you could do it."

"I did it, all right," I muttered. "But Shawna ruined the whole thing."

"What?" asked Janine. "Who's Shawna?"

I explained everything to Janine, telling her all the details of what had happened at the end of math class that day.

"But Claudia," Janine said, "why didn't you stick up for yourself?"

"I tried to," I wailed. "Mr. Zorzi just didn't give me a chance. He's not a *mean* teacher — but I guess he's making certain assumptions. He doesn't know me *or* Shawna that well."

Janine shook her head slowly. "What a mess," she said.

"I know," I answered. "And the worst thing is that I'm sure that Shawna must have cheated. But I can't figure out *why* she did — and I have no way to prove it!"

"Think back," said Janine. "Try to remember the day of the test. Can you picture her looking at your paper?"

I closed my eyes and tried to concentrate. But no matter how hard I tried, I couldn't remember a thing about that day. (Except for what I wore. I can always remember what I was wearing on a given day. I had decided on the ballet flats, in case you were wondering.)

"It's no use, Janine," I said. I felt so trapped. There just wasn't anything I could do about the horrible situation I was in.

"Do you have any idea why Shawna might have cheated?" asked Janine.

"That's the weird thing," I said. "She's usually a pretty good student. Something strange is going on here."

"Yes, and you've got to try to get to the bottom of it," said Janine. "But where do you start?"

Janine and I talked for a little bit longer, but we couldn't figure out any plan of action except one: study, study, study. I'd just have to be a math machine for awhile. I accepted Janine's offer of help, but I can't say I was looking forward to the rest of the year.

Later, after I'd gotten into my pajamas, I called Stacey and told her what had happened.

I gave her just the bare facts — I was too tired to go into it much more than that. She was incredibly nice about it all — that's why she's my best friend — but nothing she said could take away the awful feeling in the pit of my stomach.

As I went to bed that night, I thought about the day. The confrontation with Mr. Zorzi was one of the most terrible things I'd ever been through. Being accused of cheating was humiliating. I also felt really awful about having my wonderful A– taken away from me. And I felt guilty about taking up so much of Janine's time so that she could tutor me.

But you know what was the worst part of the whole thing? The feeling that my parents were not *one hundred percent absolutely, positively, definitely* convinced that I was telling the truth. *That* was what was making me feel so rotten.

CHAPTER 7

"I just can't believe that he would be so unfair!" said Jessi. She was sitting on the floor next to Mallory. They were both eating Fig Newtons.

"What gets me is the way he wouldn't listen to you." That was Stacey, who was sitting in my desk chair. It was clear that she'd already told everybody about my problem.

"Order!" Guess who said that? Right. Kristy. She was sitting in the director's chair, as usual, wearing her visor. And the clock next to my bed said 5:30. It was time for our club meeting to start.

"We definitely have a problem on our hands," Kristy said. "But we need to take care of club business before we get into it."

We? I thought it was *my* problem. I should have known that my friends would want to help me out. And it felt good to know that everyone was in my corner. I passed around a box of Mallomars as Kristy went through the club business. When she was finished, she said, "Okay. Now, Claudia, why don't you tell us, in your own words, what happened yesterday."

In my own words? Whose words did she think I'd use? Kristy's funny sometimes, even when she doesn't mean to be. "Well," I began, "it all started right as class was ending — "

Just then the phone rang. Kristy answered it and quickly arranged a job for Stacey with Charlotte Johanssen. I smiled at Stacey. Charlotte is her favorite kid to sit for.

Then I continued. "Mr. Zorzi called me and Shawna up to his desk. I didn't know what was going on!"

The phone rang again. Mrs. Braddock needed a sitter for Matt and Haley. Mary Anne checked the record book to see who was free that afternoon, and Jessi got the job. She's the best of all of us at sign language, so as long as she's free, she's usually the first choice to sit for them. Matt's deaf, but he's a pro in sign language. We've all learned a little.

"So, where was I?" I asked after the job had been arranged. I continued with my story, embellishing it with all the details I remembered.

Even though I was interrupted three more times by phone calls, I finally got to the end of it.

"Why did Mr. Zorzi have to be so mean?" asked Mallory. She really looked upset.

Dawn looked upset, too. "He's just making assumptions, and that's not right," she said.

Then Mary Anne spoke up. Very softly, she said, "You know, Claud, if you *did* look at Shawna's paper, we'd stand right behind you anyway." I looked at her, amazed. I couldn't believe my ears. She went on. "If you did it, you should confess. You'll feel better, and we'll still be here for you."

The room was completely quiet for about five seconds. Everybody looked stunned. Then Kristy spoke up.

"Mary Anne, how *could* you? Of *course* Claudia didn't do it. You must be crazy."

Mary Anne looked around the room. We were all glaring at her. She burst into tears. (I told you she was sensitive.)

I reached over and hugged her. "That's okay, Mary Anne. I know you were trying to be supportive. But I'd rather you just believe me," I said.

The tears were over almost as soon as they'd

begun. "I do, Claud, I do!" she said. "I just wanted you to know that it wouldn't matter to any of us if — "

"Okay, Mary Anne, enough of that," interrupted Kristy. "Now, look," she went on. "Let's go over the whole thing again. We've got to figure out how to prove that Claud is innocent."

"Well, it's obvious that Shawna was the one who cheated," said Mallory. "So all we need to do is figure out how to prove it."

"But why would Shawna cheat?" asked Stacey. "She always gets good grades. Why would she risk being caught?"

"Forget about Shawna for a minute," said Kristy. "What about Mr. Zorzi? How can we convince him that it's wrong to consider Claudia guilty without proof?"

"My parents wanted to go to school and talk to the principal," I admitted. "But I wouldn't let them."

"No, I think it's best if we handle this ourselves," said Kristy. "Do you think Janine would have any ideas? She's such a genius — maybe *she* can figure this out."

I shook my head, just as the phone rang again. Janine and I had been over all the angles already. If she hadn't thought of something last night . . .

Kristy put her hand over the mouthpiece of the phone. "Claud," she said. "Do you want to sit for the Perkinses on Friday? They asked especially for you."

That was nice of Kristy. Usually the jobs are given out very fairly, and we try not to let clients get too attached to any one sitter. I guess this time Kristy figured I might need the distraction of sitting for Myriah and Gabbie and their baby sister, Laura Elizabeth.

"Sure," I said. "Sounds great."

Kristy finished with Mrs. Perkins and hung up.

"You don't sound all that excited about the job," said Kristy.

"It's just that . . ." I started. I could hardly bring myself to say it. "I'm afraid that if I fail math, my parents will make me quit the club."

A silence fell over the room.

"Okay, that's it," said Dawn. "We're going to get to the bottom of this. No way are we going to lose you!"

"Think, Claud," said Jessi. "Isn't there any way we can prove that Shawna cheated?"

"But that's just the thing," I said. "Maybe

she didn't. Maybe Mr. Zorzi was wrong. Maybe it was just a coincidence that we got the same problems wrong — in the same way."

Stacey was shaking her head. "No, Claud," she said. "He was right. It would have been one thing if you both just missed the same questions. But it's another thing entirely for you to have come up with the exact same wrong answers. There's hardly any chance of that happening by coincidence."

"That's what Mr. Zorzi told us," I said sadly. Stacey's such a math whiz. If she said the same thing that Mr. Zorzi did, it must be true.

"You know," said Dawn, as if she were thinking out loud, "Shawna and some of her friends are in my homeroom. They've been acting kind of strange lately."

"You're right!" said Mary Anne (She's in the same homeroom as Dawn.) "They've been passing notes a lot and acting like they know it all."

"Boy, speaking of Shawna's friends, did you see Susan Taylor yesterday?" asked Dawn. "She got another perm, and this one's really wild."

"I heard that her mother writes her a note

to get out of classes when she has a hair appointment," said Kristy. "Can you imagine?"

"I know," said Stacey. "I told my mom about that. She said if I thought she'd do that for me I had 'another think coming.' "

"Okay, you guys," said Mary Anne. She doesn't like to gossip as much as the rest of us do. She thinks it's mean. "Let's get back to the problem. How are we going to prove that Shawna cheated and that Claudia is innocent?"

Everybody was quiet for a few minutes. Then the phone rang. I almost jumped out of my skin! This time Stacey took the call and arranged an afternoon job for Mallory, sitting for Jamie Newton while Mrs. Newton took the baby (Lucy Jane) to the pediatrician.

I guess Dawn had been thinking the whole time that Stacey was handling the call, because as soon as Stacey hung up the phone, she started to talk. "You know," she said, "Shawna's locker is right next to mine."

"So?" asked Kristy.

"Well, I'm just wondering . . ." said Dawn slowly. "Suppose one of those notes she and her friends keep passing said something incriminating about her cheating."

"And?" asked Kristy again. She usually thinks so fast. I could see that she was a little impatient with Dawn.

"Well, I happen to know Shawna's locker combination. There was a mix-up, and I had that locker for a couple of weeks when school started. Then we switched."

"Dawn Schafer!" said Mary Anne in a shocked voice. "Are you saying that someone should *break into* Shawna's locker to look for a note?"

"It's a thought," said Dawn calmly.

"Boy, I don't know about that," said Stacey. "That would be kind of like breaking the law or something, wouldn't it?"

"Not really," said Dawn. "We wouldn't be *stealing* anything. We'd just be looking for evidence."

"Don't you need a search warrant for that kind of thing?" asked Mallory.

"You've been watching too many detective shows on TV," I answered. "Dawn's talking about looking for a note in a locker, not looking for a loaded pistol or something!" The idea was growing on me. "I think it might just work!"

"Well, we can think about it," said Kristy.

"But there must be some other way — a safer way — to prove that Shawna cheated."

Kristy was probably right. But unfortunately, we didn't come up with any brilliant ideas by the time that day's meeting was over.

CHAPTER 8

Thursday

Hey Mal, do me a favor.

what, Jessi?

Well, when I grow up, and I'm ready to have children, just remind me.

Remind you to what?

Remind me to never have triplets.

Right, Jessi.

I can't really blame Jessi for feeling a little down on triplets. She'd had kind of a rough afternoon with Adam, Jordan, and Byron. Jessi had been right on time that afternoon for the job of helping Mal sit for her brothers and sisters. (Mrs. Pike always insists on two sitters when all the Pike kids are home, and that's fine with us. It would be next to impossible to watch all seven of them if you were alone!)

"The triplets are still grounded, Jessi," said Mrs. Pike as she got her coat from the hall closet. "That means they aren't allowed out of the house. They don't have to stay in their room, but they can't go outside. And they aren't allowed to get or make any phone calls."

Jessi remembered the story that Stacey had written up in the club notebook. "You mean they still won't tell who broke the window?" she asked.

"That's right," said Mrs. Pike. "I can't believe they're being so loyal to each other." She lowered her voice and went on. "I almost hate to keep punishing them — after all, that kind of loyalty is a good thing — but I have to be consistent with them. Anyway, it can't go on much longer."

Jessi nodded. She had already started to

work on a plan. Maybe she could get the triplets to spill the beans!

"I've got to run," said Mrs. Pike. "Mallory and the kids are in the kitchen, having a snack. Have a good afternoon!"

Jessi said good-bye to Mrs. Pike and walked into the kitchen. The scene there was completely chaotic. Mallory was standing in the middle of the kitchen looking like a traffic cop who had lost control. Margo and Claire were sitting at the table, giggling as they peeled grapes and fed them to Nicky, who was acting like a movie monster.

"Ummm," he said. "Delicious eyeballs. Norkon like eyeballs. Feed Norkon more!"

Vanessa was staring dreamily into the refrigerator, trying to decide on a snack. (The Pike kids are allowed to eat anything they want, by the way. Mr. and Mrs. Pike figured that if they argued over every bite of food that eight kids were eating, they'd have no time left to do anything else.)

"Carrot, apple, cottage cheese — which of these will truly please?" she rhymed.

"Vanessa, forget the poetry. Make up your mind and close the refrigerator," Mallory said. "You know Mom doesn't like us to stand there with the door open."

"You know Mom doesn't like us to stand there with the door open," said Adam, mimicking Mallory.

"Oh, cut it out," said Mallory. I could tell that she was feeling the effects of having the triplets cooped up inside for a few days.

"Oh, cut it out," said all three triplets at once.

Mallory glared at the triplets, who were sitting on the countertop, eating peanut-butter-and-salami sandwiches and kicking their heels against the cabinet.

"Stop it. Now. And get down from there this minute!" said Mallory. She was losing her temper.

"Stop it —" began the triplets, but Jessi cut them off. This was getting out of hand.

"Come on, guys," she said. "That's enough."

I don't know why they listened to Jessi — maybe because she's not their big sister. But the triplets slid off the counter and sat down at the table. Jessi and Mallory exchanged glances and Mallory gave a sigh of relief.

Just then, the phone rang. Vanessa grabbed it. "This is the Pikes'," she said. "Whom would you like?"

Honestly. When she gets started with that rhyming thing, there's no stopping her.

"It's for you, Adam," she said. "Somebody wants to know if you'd like to play baseball."

"*Would* I!" yelled Adam, lunging for the phone.

"Hold it, buddy!" said Mallory. "No way. Number one, you can't leave the house. Number two, you're not allowed to use the phone, remember?"

"Number three, you're a nerd," said Adam under his breath.

Mallory bristled and Jessi could see that she was on the verge of losing her cool completely.

"Mal," she said, "how about if you take the younger kids outside to play? I'll stay inside with the triplets."

Mallory gave Jessi a grateful look. "Oh, that would be terrific," she said. "They've been like this for the last few days, and I just can't take it anymore. They're like caged beasts or something!" Within minutes, she'd herded Nicky, Vanessa, Margo, and Claire outside.

Jessi started to tidy up the kitchen, which looked like a tornado had been through it, while the boys played in the living room. She could hear them talking as they looked through their baseball cards for the millionth time.

"Ave-day Infield-way," said Jordan. "E's-hay the oolest-cay."

"O-nay ay-way," cried Adam. "At-whay about-hay Al-cay Ipken-ray Unior-jay?"

Byron (who isn't as much into sports as the other two) spoke up. "I-hay ike-lay Agic-may Ohnson-jay."

The other two triplets sat in amazed silence for about two seconds. Then Jordan spoke up. "I-hay ike-lay Agic-may, oo-tay, ummy-day. Ut-bay e-hay ays-play asketball-bay!" He and Adam snickered.

"Orget-fay about-hay ese-thay ards-cay. I'm-hay ick-say of-hay em-thay," said Adam. "Et's-lay eak-snay outside-hay!"

Jessi poked her head into the room. She was getting a little tired of hearing Pig Latin, and she didn't like the way Jordan had spoken to his brother. Byron is sensitive, and his feelings get hurt easily. Besides, she wasn't about to let the triplets sneak out of the house.

"Ordan-jay, at-thay isn't-hay ery-vay ice-nay. Ell-tay our-yay other-bray ou're-yay orry-say or-fay alling-cay im-hay ummy-day!"

All three triplets stared at Jessi, gaping in disbelief. "You know how to speak Pig Latin?" asked Adam.

"Sure!" said Jessi. "I used to talk that way all the time. Sometimes I get sick of it, though."

"We get kind of tired of it, too," admitted Adam. "But we've got to have a secret language for when we don't want anybody to understand us."

"Pig Latin's too common, though," said Jessi. "Lots of people know how to speak Pig Latin. Bop-u-top nop-o-bop-o-dop-yop kop-nop-o-wop-sop hop-o-wop top-o sop-pop-e-a-kop 'op-talk.' "

"Whaaaat?" asked the triplets in unison.

"That's 'op-talk,' " said Jessi.

"Teach us!" demanded Jordan.

"Yeah! Teach us!" said Adam and Byron.

"What do you say?" asked Jessi, teasing them.

"Please?" said the triplets.

Jessi sat down on the floor with the boys and told them about 'op-talk.' "It's simple," she said. "You just spell out each word, but you add 'op' after every consonant."

"What about the vowels?" asked Byron.

"You leave those alone," said Jessi. "So if you wanted to say, 'I want to go home' in 'op-talk,' you'd just say 'I wop-a-nop-top top-o-gop-o — "

"Hop-o-mop-e!" yelled Adam. "I get it!"

Jordan was frowning slightly. "What about 'y'?" he asked.

"You treat 'y' like a consonant," said Jessi.

"O-kop-a-yop!" said Jordan. "Top-hop-i-sop i-sop gop-rop-e-a-top!"

"Say my name, Jessi!" said Byron. He still wasn't getting the hang of it.

"Bop-yop-rop-o-nop!" said Jessi, Adam, and Jordan all together. Then they burst out laughing. Byron's name really sounded funny.

"Do mine!" yelled Adam.

This time Byron joined in, too. "A-dop-a-mop!" they yelled. The triplets dissolved in giggles. 'Op-talk' was a big hit.

Jessi sat back and let the triplets go at it. They were fast learners. After they'd done everybody's name, they started to plan how to best use 'op-talk' to annoy their parents. They decided to speak nothing but 'op-talk' at dinner that night, just to see what would happen.

Jessi was happy to see that the boys had forgotten, at least for awhile, how tired they were of being in the house. They'd dropped their mean-spirited teasing. Now they were just having fun. She thought this might be a good time to bring up the subject of the broken window. Maybe she could get them to tell her which one of them had been responsible.

"So, wouldn't you guys like to be able to go outside?" she asked. "All you have to do is tell me which one of you broke that window."

The three of them sat there silently.

"Come on," said Jessi. "It's not such a big deal. Do you want to be grounded forever?"

Silence.

"Don't you want your allowances back?" she asked.

The triplets ignored her.

Jessi thought for a moment. Maybe she could trick them into exposing the guilty party. She turned to Byron, and said, very casually. "Tell me, Byron. When you threw that ball through the window — "

"I didn't!" Byron said, without thinking.

"Aha!" cried Jessi.

"I didn't, either!" said Adam and Jordan at the same time.

That was it for Jessi. She sighed in frustration and let the triplets go back to practicing 'op-talk.' If they were going to be so stubborn about it, she wasn't going to try to help anymore. It wasn't *her* problem if they wanted to be grounded until they were ninety-two years old.

CHAPTER 9

The next day in school, all my classes seemed to drag on forever. I couldn't concentrate on what my teachers were saying; I just kept thinking about my problem and how to solve it.

Then it happened.

As I was heading for the cafeteria, I saw Shawna Riverson walking in front of me. Susan Taylor was with her, and so was another friend of theirs, this girl with wild red hair. Their heads were together, and they were talking in low voices as they walked. They were giggling, too. I followed them without really knowing why.

They started to go around the corner toward the cafeteria, but then Shawna stopped and gestured towards the girls' room. She walked into it, and the other two followed her.

I stood outside the door for about thirty seconds, trying to figure out what Nancy Drew would do if she were in my shoes. Then I slowly pushed the door open and peeked inside.

There are four stalls in that bathroom. Three of them were occupied by Shawna and her friends. Quickly, before I could change my mind, I slipped into the fourth.

The toilet next to mine flushed then, and I heard someone walk over to the sink. The water ran for a minute. Then I heard a girl say, "Shawna, I swear. You are so lucky." She was chewing gum loudly. That must be the one with the red hair, I thought.

"I know," said Shawna, who had just come out of *her* stall. "I still can't believe I got away with it." She giggled. "I just gave Mr. Zorzi this incredibly sincere, honest look — and he let me go!"

I couldn't believe what I was hearing. Were they talking about what I thought they were talking about? I was suddenly terrified that they would find out I was eavesdropping on them. I held my breath and tried to get my heart to stop beating so loudly. I kept listening. This was exactly what I wanted to hear.

"And you know the best part?" asked Shawna. "I don't even have to feel bad about it. It doesn't even matter to *her* that she's getting an F. You know what I mean?"

"Yeah, what's one more bad grade to Claudia Kishi?" asked Susan Taylor.

Oh, wow. I couldn't believe she said that! Suddenly, I was furious. How *dare* they talk about me that way? My face got all hot again, just like it had that day after math class. I felt tears welling up in my eyes.

I jumped up and started to open the door of my stall. I was going to give them the shock of their lives!

Then I stopped. I can't explain why — but I cooled down as quickly as I'd gotten fired up. It was as if I felt Nancy Drew herself tapping me on the shoulder and whispering in my ear. Maybe if I kept quiet, she was saying, I'd hear some more. And maybe what I heard would help me figure out what to do next. I listened to Nancy's advice.

After all, the main thing was to prove my own innocence — not to Shawna, since she obviously already *knew* I was innocent — but to Mr. Zorzi and to the principal.

I took a few deep breaths (very *quiet* deep

breaths) and settled down to listen some more. I peeked, carefully, through the crack between the stall and the door. Shawna and her friends were still standing there, looking in the mirror and talking while they brushed their hair and made what they seemed to think were movie star faces. Susan Taylor pulled a tiny can of hairspray out of her purse and touched up her perfect perm.

"I wouldn't have done it unless I had to, you know," said Shawna. "I've never done it before."

"I know," said Susan. "But nobody could be expected to do everything you do and *also* get good grades all the time."

"I just had too much going on," said Shawna. "There was that skit I was directing for Drama Club, and that long paper for English — "

"Yeah, and then you had to help plan the Pep Rally on top of it all!" said the girl with red hair. "How were you going to find time to study for some dumb math test, too? What are you supposed to be, Supergirl or something?"

I rolled my eyes. Was I supposed to feel sorry for Shawna? I mean, give me a break.

She's the most popular girl in school! Of *course* she's too busy.

"I just figured it was too, too perfect when I heard Claudia telling mousy Mary Anne Spier that her genius sister, Janine, was helping her study," said Shawna.

"Yeah, everybody knows what a brain Janine is," answered Susan. "But who would ever suspect you of copying off of Claudia Kishi's paper? It was the perfect crime." She giggled.

This was too much. Not only had she copied off of me, but she'd planned the whole thing. And she sounded *proud* of herself.

Finally, after what seemed like hours, Shawna and her friends packed up their purses and left, letting the door slam shut behind them. I let out a big sigh and walked out of my stall. Looking at myself in the mirror, I shook my head. This was unbelievable.

I *flew* to the cafeteria to meet my friends. I couldn't wait to tell them what I'd heard.

They were already sitting down and eating by the time I got there. I skipped the line, too excited to eat. I threw myself down at the table and said, "You'll never guess what I just heard."

I looked around the table at my friends.

Mary Anne was sitting next to Logan. They had been talking quietly together, but they looked up at me as soon as I started to speak. Dawn put down her sprouts-on-cracked-wheatberry-bread sandwich (it looked disgusting) and turned to me, too. Kristy and Stacey were all ears. (Jessi and Mallory weren't there — the sixth-graders eat during another period.)

I turned and checked over my shoulder, just to make sure that Shawna and her friends weren't standing behind me. Then I told the whole story from beginning to end.

Kristy got furious. "That . . . that *dirty rotten cheater!*" she sputtered.

Mary Anne felt sorry for me, I could tell. "That must have been horrible, to hear them saying those things about you," she said. "That's so mean!"

Stacey just gave me a sympathetic look. Then she smiled. "But Claud — now you have proof, right?"

"I wish," I said. "But even though I know for sure now that Shawna cheated, I still can't prove it." I bit my lip and shook my head. "If I tried to tell that to Mr. Zorzi, it would just be my word against Shawna's —and we know who *he'd* believe."

Logan nodded. "Claudia's right," he said. "So what do we do?" I guess Mary Anne had filled him in on the details. It was nice to know that I had one more person on my side.

Dawn hadn't said anything yet, but just then she spoke up. "So Claud has solved the mystery of who really cheated — and why. Now we have to figure out how to help Mr. Zorzi and the principal solve the same mystery." She paused for a minute, then spoke again, in a lower voice. "We could always try what I thought of the other day," she said. "You know — we could check Shawna's locker."

I noticed that she wasn't using the term "break into" anymore.

Mary Anne looked shocked. "Dawn!" she whispered, looking around the cafeteria. "Shhh! Don't talk about that here. Somebody might hear you and take you seriously."

"I am serious," said Dawn, more quietly. "I think it's our only chance."

"I don't believe you," said Mary Anne. "The whole idea is just unthinkable."

"I kind of agree with Mary Anne," said Stacey quietly. "I'd do almost anything to help you prove you're innocent, Claud." She looked over at me. "*Almost* anything. But not that. That's going too far."

I had to admit that Stacey was right, kind of. But what else could we do?

"Wait a minute," said Kristy. "Do you guys want Claud to have to quit the club?"

Stacey put her hand over her mouth. "Oh!" she said. "I wasn't thinking about that."

Mary Anne frowned. "Of course we don't want to lose Claudia. But there must be a better way of keeping her in the club."

Kristy sat up straight in her chair and pounded her fist on the table. "You know what Watson would say in a case like this? He'd say, 'Desperate times call for desperate measures!'"

I looked at her. What on earth was she talking about?

She must have seen that I was confused. "It just means that some things are emergencies, and that during an emergency you have to do things you might not otherwise do," she explained.

I nodded. I agreed completely. When I looked over at Stacey, she was nodding, too.

"You're right, Kristy," she said. "I think we should do it. And I'll be glad to help, if it means keeping Claudia in the club."

Dawn was grinning now.

Mary Anne was the only one of us who wasn't totally convinced. She still looked worried. "I think it's wrong," she said. "But if you have to do it, please be careful. Imagine what could happen if you got caught!"

CHAPTER 10

I didn't *want* to imagine what would happen if we got caught "checking" Shawna's locker — so I just didn't think about it. Instead, I joined my friends in planning exactly how to go about doing the deed.

The five of us spent the rest of lunch period talking about it. (Logan had left by then — I don't think he wanted to be involved in our plan.)

"I happen to know that the Pep Squad has a meeting after school this afternoon — at three o'clock," I said. "Susan Taylor mentioned it when they were in the girls' room. She was worried that it would go past four o'clock and she'd miss the chance to go shopping with her mom."

"Is that all she ever does — shop and get perms?" asked Kristy.

"Seems like it," said Dawn. "Anyway, this

meeting is perfect. By three o'clock, most of the other kids in school will have left — or else they'll be involved in some activity."

"But what about the teachers?" I asked, picturing Mr. Zorzi strolling up behind me as I rummaged through Shawna's locker. "Won't they still be around?"

Dawn wasn't fazed. "Sure. But they don't know whose locker is whose."

"Mr. Kingbridge knows," said Mary Anne. "He knows every little thing about this school." (Mr. Kingbridge is the vice-principal.)

"Oh, him," said Dawn. "He's half-blind." Mary Anne gasped, then giggled, covering her mouth with her hand. "Anyway," continued Dawn, "he'll just figure I'm at *my* locker. All we have to do this afternoon is stand in front of Shawna's locker as if it were mine, and laugh and talk as we go through it for evidence."

Dawn was really into it. I was glad she'd decided that she would be the one to go through Shawna's locker. I still felt a little uneasy about the whole thing, even if it *was* my only chance.

Mary Anne felt uneasy, too. "What if *Shawna* catches you?" she asked.

"She's going to be at practice, Mary Anne,"

said Kristy patiently. Mary Anne can be such a worrier.

"But what if she forgets something and comes back for it?" said Mary Anne.

Hmmmm. That made us all stop and think. Mary Anne had a point. We sure didn't want to be caught in the act by the owner of the locker.

"No problem," Stacey said after a minute. "I'll stand guard where the two hallways meet. If I see her coming, I'll warn you."

"Great!" said Dawn. "And don't forget to watch out for Susan Taylor and that redhead, too."

Just then, the bell rang. Lunch period was over.

It's funny about time. Remember how I said that my morning classes seemed to go on forever? Well, that afternoon, when I really wasn't looking forward to school being over (I was *so* nervous about what we were going to do), my classes flew by. Before I knew it, the last bell had rung.

I met my friends by my locker — we'd planned it that way. By then, Mallory and Jessi had heard about our plan. They were as excited as the rest of us.

"You guys should go on home," said Dawn

to Mal and Jessi. "If we get caught, we don't want you to be involved."

"That's right," I said. "Mary Anne, you should go, too. We'll tell you all about it later."

Stacey agreed with me. "Good plan," she said. "Kristy, you'd better leave with them, too. The fewer of us that are involved, the better."

Once the four of them had left, it was just a matter of waiting until three o'clock rolled around. That sounds simple but it wasn't.

The minutes seemed to stretch on forever. At first, there were a lot of kids in the halls. But after the buses left, the school grew quiet. Kids walked by themselves or in pairs, heading to things like Spanish Club or soccer practice. We didn't see Shawna and her friends at all.

First we hung around my locker for awhile. Then Stacey realized she'd forgotten her jacket, so we headed over to her locker. We got the jacket, but it still wasn't three o'clock.

The water fountain kept us busy for a couple of minutes — but how much water can you drink? I wasn't thirsty anyway. I was just a nervous wreck. This phrase kept going through my mind: "Breaking and Entering." That was what the newspaper called it when somebody got arrested for burglary. Was "Breaking and Entering" what we were planning?

After the water fountain, we headed for the girls' room. We didn't want to hang out in any one place too long, in case Mr. Kingbridge noticed and got suspicious.

Being in the girls' room made me remember all those nasty things Shawna and her friends had said about me. I got mad all over again, which was probably good — it kept me from being too nervous.

Finally, it was three o'clock. We stepped out into the hall. It was empty. "Okay, this is it!" said Dawn. "Stacey, man your post."

"Don't you mean 'woman' my post?" said Stacey, giggling. Dawn gave her a Look.

"Come on, Stacey. This is serious," she said. "Now don't forget — come running if you spot Shawna or any of her friends. Or Mr. Kingbridge, for that matter!"

"Check!" said Stacey, giving Dawn a mock salute. Then she wished us luck and headed down the hall.

A few moments later, Dawn and I were standing in front of Shawna's locker. Dawn looked around and then bent over the dial. She twisted it a few times and tried the latch.

Whooosh! The locker opened and an avalanche of stuff fell out. Crumpled-up papers, stuffed notebooks, old chewed-up pens . . . and a picture of the most gorgeous guy I'd ever seen.

"Who's *that?*" I asked, grabbing it.

"Come on, Claud," said Dawn. "This is no time for boy-watching. Quick! Put it back before somebody comes."

She was right. I got down on the floor, grabbed a handful of papers, and shoved them back into the locker. Boy, Shawna was a slob! I tried to check through the papers as I put them away, but nothing interesting was written on them.

"Check the shelf," said Dawn.

I nodded and stood on my tiptoes to see what was up there. "A bathing suit, a hairbrush, a copy of the school manual . . ." Pretty boring, I thought. "And what's this? Ew! A gross, old, moldy orange!" I pulled my hand away from it.

"Shhhh!" said Dawn. "Who's coming?"

I listened and heard footsteps. They were coming closer. Dawn and I tried to act casual. "So, did you understand the assignment for English class?" I asked.

Dawn and I aren't even in the same English class, but I don't think the janitor knew. That's who was coming. He walked by, pushing a cart. He didn't give us a second look.

"Okay, let's get serious," said Dawn. "Look for a note." She bent over and started rummaging around in the papers that covered the bottom of Shawna's locker.

For some reason, I looked at the inside of the locker door. Shawna had all the usual stuff — a mirror, some stickers, some posters of cute boys — but there, stuck in the vent — what was that? I pulled out a folded-up piece of pink paper. A note. "Dawn, listen to what this says," I said.

" 'Congratulations on your A–. Who would have guessed that C.K.'s paper would have had so many right answers?' "

C.K. That was me. Evidence! I stuffed the note into my pocket, and Dawn slammed the locker shut. We ran down the hall, grabbed Stacey, and then leaned against the wall, panting. Victory!

Then I had a terrible thought. The note wasn't worth a thing. If I showed it to Mr. Zorzi or the principal, they'd want to know where I got it. And if I wouldn't tell them (which I couldn't), why should they believe that Shawna's friend even wrote it?

"Why don't you guys go on," I said to Dawn

and Stacey after I'd told them what I'd realized. "I just remembered a book I need from my locker."

When they'd left, I headed for Shawna's locker and stuck the note into the vent. It wasn't going to do me any good, and by putting it back I felt a little less guilty about what we'd done.

I also felt pretty low. Now we were really at a dead end. It looked like I was just going to have to accept that F.

"Y ou *what?*" asked Dawn. "I can't believe you put that note back!"

It was lunchtime, the day after we'd tried Breaking and Entering into Shawna's locker. Dawn had been telling everybody the details of what we'd done and what we'd found. Then I spoke up and told them how I'd put the note back.

"After all that!" said Stacey. "Oh, well, I guess you're right. You couldn't really have used it for evidence without incriminating yourself."

"That's true," said Kristy. "But boy, I wish I could have seen Shawna's face if you had confronted her with that note!" She shook her head.

Mary Anne looked at me and smiled. "You did the right thing, Claud," she said softly. "I'm proud of you."

"*I* may have done the right thing," I said. "But Shawna didn't. And I still need to prove it." I frowned down at my disgusting-looking Sloppy Joe. "I just can't think of anything else to do, though. I'm stuck."

For a few minutes nobody said anything. It seemed like we were *all* stuck. I felt miserable.

"And on top of everything else," I said, breaking the silence, "I have a math quiz coming up. What if I don't get an A on it?" I couldn't even think about what might happen if I started to fail math.

"Don't worry, Claud," said Stacey. "I'll help you study. You can get all A's if we work hard enough." She stopped to think for a moment. "But you know, maybe you should ask Mr. Zorzi if you can sit in a different seat on the day of the test. We wouldn't want the whole thing to start all over again."

She had a point. Shawna had done it once — why wouldn't she do it again? "Okay, you're right," I said. "I'll ask him. But we still haven't figured out how to prove that Shawna was the cheater instead of me."

"I've got it!" said Kristy. She'd been quiet for a few minutes, and she must have been thinking hard. "Remember how we tricked Cokie Gray into incriminating herself?"

94

"Yeah!" said Dawn. "That's right. Remember when she was pretending to be Kristy's mystery admirer? We finally tricked her into admitting that she was the one sending all those weird notes."

"That's not the only time we tricked Cokie," said Mary Anne. "Remember when she was trying to make us believe that there was a bad-luck curse on me?"

"That's right," said Kristy, grinning. "She walked straight into our trap." She rubbed her hands together. "And if it worked on Cokie, it'll work on Shawna."

"Right!" said Stacey, beaming at me. "We'll just let Shawna do the work of proving her own guilt."

I nodded slowly. "Okay," I said. "I'll try anything at this point."

"Now all you have to do is figure out how to set her up in front of Mr. Zorzi," said Mary Anne, just as the bell rang. Lunch period was over.

The chalk screeched on the blackboard as Mr. Zorzi drew a complicated-looking diagram. It was Monday and math class was just about to begin. I'd spent practically the whole weekend trying to think up traps for Shawna to fall into, but I hadn't come up with much. Still, I was eager to get going.

I decided to start right away. My first idea was to try to nudge Shawna into confessing by using certain meaningful words — words that would let her know that I was "onto her game," as they say in the detective movies.

"Oh!" I said, looking into my notebook. "I can't find my *copy* of that last handout." As I said the word *copy* I looked at Shawna. "Does anyone else have a *copy* I can borrow?" I asked. "I'd hate to *cheat* Mr. Zorzi out of another one."

Shawna was looking back at me with a puzzled expression. Some of the other kids in class were giving me funny looks, too.

I hardly noticed their glances. I was on a roll. "Can I just *steal* your *copy* for a minute, Shawna?" I said. "I really need it — and that's no *lie*."

I'd expected Shawna to break down and confess when she heard all those incriminating words. But she was looking at me as if I'd gone crazy. "Sure, you can borrow it," she said, bending over to search through her backpack. "But I don't think we're going to need it today."

I was disappointed. Shawna didn't seem to

be getting the messages I was sending to her. I guess she just didn't feel all that guilty about what she'd done. It wasn't going to be easy to make her crack.

"Here, Claudia," said Shawna, reaching over to give me the handout.

"Oh, never mind," I said.

"Claudia! Shawna!" said Mr. Zorzi. "Are you ready to get started?" I'd been so involved in carrying out my plan to trap Shawna that I hadn't noticed him standing in front of the class, ready to begin.

"Yes, Mr. Zorzi," I said. Shawna was still sitting there with the paper in her hand. She raised her eyebrows at me and shook her head. Then she put the handout away.

"Yes, Mr. Zorzi," she echoed.

Oh, my lord. I had really been expecting that plan to work. Maybe it would have, if I had been able to keep it up long enough. I hadn't really come up with too many other ideas for trapping Shawna. What was I going to do next?

Mr. Zorzi droned on about "whole numbers." He wasn't making a lot of sense — but then, I wasn't paying that much attention to him. I was thinking hard.

How could I prove that Shawna had copied

off of my paper? First, I decided, I'd have to show that it was possible for her to read my answers from where she sat. But what was I going to do, give her an eye test?

Suddenly, out of nowhere, the answer popped into my mind. I thought of this bumper sticker I'd seen once on an old junky car on the highway. "IF YOU CAN READ THIS, YOU'RE TOO CLOSE!" The sticker was printed in pretty small letters, so that you wouldn't be able to read it unless you were right behind the other car.

I looked down at my notebook. So far I hadn't taken any notes on Mr. Zorzi's lecture. Guess what I wrote across the page. I wrote it in letters about the same size as my regular writing, so it would make a good test of Shawna's vision. Here's what it said: "IF YOU CAN READ THIS, YOU ARE A CHEATER AND YOU MIGHT AS WELL ADMIT IT!"

I looked at it and almost burst out laughing. This *had* to work. Now I just had to wait for Shawna to notice what I'd written. When she read it (and I was sure she'd be able to) her face would turn all red and she'd probably say something incriminating.

There was only one problem. Unlike me, Shawna was paying attention to Mr. Zorzi.

She was taking notes on everything he said. She had no reason to look over at me — or my paper.

I had to get her attention. First, I cleared my throat. "Ahem!" I said, loudly. She didn't look. I tapped my pen against my desk, hoping that she'd turn to see where the noise was coming from. She seemed absorbed in her note taking.

"Pssst . . . Shawna!" I whispered, as quietly as I could. She didn't seem to hear me.

I'd caught the attention of some of the other kids in class, though. They were looking at me, watching to see what I would do next.

Desperate times call for desperate measures, I thought. I gave a *huge* yawn, stretching my arms over my head.

"Claudia Kishi!" said Mr. Zorzi. "What on earth are you doing?"

Ooops. I'd gotten kind of carried away and forgotten where I was.

"Sorry, Mr. Zorzi," I said, giving him my best smile.

"I suppose you know all about the whole numbers," said Mr. Zorzi, "and you don't need to review this material with the rest of us."

Yikes. That brought me back to earth. After

all, even if I could prove that Shawna was guilty, I still needed to keep up with my class. And I wasn't doing a very good job of it that day.

"Yes, Mr. Zorzi," I said without thinking. "I mean, no, Mr. Zorzi," I said, correcting myself. "I'll pay attention. I'm sorry."

I heard some giggles behind me. I turned to see who was laughing, and saw one of the kids making the "she's nuts!" sign and pointing at me.

Better get a grip, Claud, I thought. My plans were not working out the way they were supposed to. I decided to give up and listen to Mr. Zorzi instead. I figured I might as well get *something* out of that day's class.

I turned to a fresh page in my notebook and then looked over at Shawna's desk to check on what notes she'd taken so far. Then it hit me. Of course! All I had to do to prove that she could read *my* paper was to prove that I could read *hers!*

I leaned over just a bit so I could see more clearly. She was scribbling away. I caught a few words: "So then he said, 'Well, I heard that Susan told Jason that you were going to ask me to the dance.' And so I said . . ."

Wow. Shawna wasn't taking notes on what Mr. Zorzi was saying. All this time she'd been *writing* notes — to her friend!

And it looked like juicy stuff. I leaned over again to read some more. ". . . but Susan said that Jason said I had really nice hair . . ."

I was totally absorbed in what I was reading. I didn't even hear Mr. Zorzi call my name this time, but he must have been trying to get my attention for quite awhile. Just as I was getting to a really good part of Shawna's note, I felt a hand on my shoulder. I must have jumped about six feet straight up out of my seat.

"Claudia," said Mr. Zorzi, shaking his head. I looked up at him with my mouth open. I couldn't think of a thing to say. I couldn't believe I had been caught in the act, doing what I'd been trying so hard to catch Shawna doing.

Just then, the bell rang. I was in luck — math class was over.

CHAPTER 12

Tuesday

mal, your brillyunt. I can't beleive you got the trippleto "ungrounded."

<u>Something</u> had to be done. They were driving the rest of us absolutely batty.

I can see why. Iive nevver seen three boys in a werse mood. When I got too youire house, they dint even act glad to see me.

Try not to take it personally, Claudia. They were just so tired of being cooped up. But theyire definitely feeling better now.'

Mallory and I were sitting for her brothers and sisters that afternoon and you can't imagine what a bad mood the triplets were in. They still wouldn't tell which of them had broken the window, and they were still grounded. They hadn't been outside, they hadn't seen their friends, and they weren't allowed to use the phone. When I reached the Pikes' house, they barely said hello.

Being grounded wasn't what was bothering the triplets — it was the fact that they weren't even earning any allowance money. And no allowance money meant no baseball cards, no candy bars, no comic books . . . "Not even a single piece of bubble gum!" Adam wailed, telling me about it.

I was sympathetic, but as baby-sitters we had to enforce Mrs. Pike's rules. And the triplets weren't happy about that. They were sick of being inside, sick of Pig Latin, even sick of that "op-talk" Jessi had taught them — they were sick of just about everything. So I'll admit that I was pretty happy when Mallory suggested that I take the younger Pikes outside to play.

"I'll keep an eye on the triplets, Claud," she said. "I'm working on an idea that might solve the problem. And the problem *has* to be solved — or else *I* might go crazy."

"Fine with me, Mal," I said. I rounded up the rest of the kids and headed outside. Then Mallory went to work on the triplets.

Adam, Jordan, and Byron were lounging around the living room, listlessly playing with their Matchbox car collection. Mallory sat down and watched for a few minutes, ignoring the bored looks they gave her. By this time she'd gotten used to their foul mood.

"I've got an idea, guys," she said.

"Oh yeah?" asked Adam.

"So what?" asked Jordan.

"Big deal," said Byron.

"Oh, okay," said Mallory. "I guess you don't want to hear how you might be able to get ungrounded and get your allowances back. Fine with me!" And she got up to leave the room.

"Wait a minute!" said the boys at once. They begged her to tell them her idea.

"You know those reenactments you see on TV?" she asked. "Sometimes when they act out the crime it suddenly becomes obvious that the innocent-seeming person was guilty all along."

The triplets nodded.

104

"Well, how about if we reenact *this* crime?" Mal asked.

The triplets looked doubtful.

"It may be your only chance," said Mallory.

The triplets exchanged glances.

"How do we start?" asked Jordan.

Mallory told them that they should do everything possible to re-create the day that the window had been broken. "Think about that day. Try to remember everything about it," she said.

The triplets were quiet for a moment, thinking. Then they had a quick, hushed discussion. Adam turned to Mallory. "Wait here," he said. The boys ran upstairs, and when they came back down, Mallory burst out laughing. They had changed into the same clothes they'd been wearing on the day the window had been broken!

"Okay, guys," she said. "Now I know Mom said you couldn't go outside, but I think it's time to make an exception to the rule. After all, how can we reenact the crime unless we're at the scene of the crime itself?"

The boys grabbed their baseball equipment and followed Mallory outside. "Whoops!" said Byron, when they'd reached the backyard. "Forgot my batting glove!" He ran back inside.

"He didn't *really* forget it," said Jordan. "He's just re-creating. On the day the window broke, he really did forget his glove. So he's doing it again."

Mallory rolled her eyes. She could see that the triplets were going to take this to the limit. And she was right. They seemed to think that every single thing they'd done that day was important. Adam even remembered every dumb knock-knock joke he'd told.

Finally the boys got around to reenacting what they'd each been doing when the ball went through the window. And, as Mallory told me later, she saw right away whose fault it was — "everybody's and nobody's."

What happened that day (as reenacted by the triplets) was this: Jordan was pitching, Byron was at bat, and Adam was behind him, catching. (No one was fielding.)

Jordan pitched kind of a wild pitch, way up in the air and "outside." Byron swung at it, even though he should have let it go by. It glanced off his bat, and he saw that it was going toward the house. He yelled to Adam to catch it, but Adam misjudged the direction of the ball and ran the wrong way. Then the ball crashed through the basement window. And you know the rest of the story.

Mallory said she was relieved to have finally found out what had happened — and she said the triplets seemed happy to let the story out. They'd kept it quiet for so long.

She and the triplets joined me and the younger Pikes, and we played together in the yard until Mrs. Pike came home. As soon as she pulled into the driveway, Mallory ran to her.

The triplets performed their reenactment again, this time in front of all their brothers and sisters *and* their mother. Nobody had to explain anything to Mrs. Pike — she saw right away that the accident hadn't really been anybody's fault.

"Adam," she said. "Byron. Jordan!" They gathered around her. "You are now officially 'ungrounded!' " The triplets cheered and gave each other the high five. Then they turned to Mallory.

"Thanks, Mal!" shouted Byron.

"You saved us!" said Adam.

"You're the greatest!" said Jordan, hugging Mal so tightly that her face turned red. The reenactment had been a success.

That night, after dinner, I went into Janine's room and asked her if she had time to talk.

She turned off her computer right away and listened while I told her *everything* about what had been going on in school.

I told her about the conversation I'd over-heard in the bathroom. I told her about how Dawn and I had "checked" Shawna's locker. I even told her about the dumb tricks I'd used to try to get Shawna to break down and confess.

Janine listened to everything I said without making comments. All she said was "Yes?" and "Then what happened?" She was being really cool about it, and I was glad.

Then I told her what Mallory had done with the triplets that day. She laughed at first, but then she started nodding, as if she understood completely.

"So do you think it would work for me?" I asked her hopefully.

"Would *what* work, Claud?" she asked. I guess she hadn't followed my train of thought.

"A reenactment!" I said. I was excited. It seemed like a great idea to me. "We get Mr. Zorzi to let me and Shawna reenact taking the test! Then he'll see right away what hap-pened."

"Slow down, Claud." said Janine. "You're

108

forgetting something very obvious here. All Shawna would have to do is pretend not to cheat!"

I felt so dumb. How could I have missed that? There was no way Shawna would incriminate herself in a reenactment. She'd had no problem lying to Mr. Zorzi in the first place. And I had to admit she was a good actress. She'd convinced him right away that she was innocent.

What a stupid idea that reenactment had been. It was becoming obvious to me by now that I'd never be able to prove my innocence.

"This has been really hard on you, hasn't it, Claudia?" Janine asked me gently.

I looked at her and nodded, gulping back my tears.

"Don't worry," she said. "Shawna's not going to get away with making you look like a cheater."

Janine was smiling secretly, as if she were figuring something out. But I was sure that even Janine couldn't solve my problem. I shrugged. "It doesn't really matter anymore," I said.

Then I told Janine that I was going to bed,

and we said good night. Or at least *I* said good night. Janine looked as if she were off in some other world. I doubt that she even noticed when I left. She was just sitting there, smiling to herself.

CHAPTER 13

"It doesn't really matter anymore." That's what I had said to Janine, and that's what I had to make myself believe. Maybe I could do a really good job of acting like I didn't care about being accused of cheating. If I convinced everybody else that it didn't matter anymore, maybe I would start to believe it, too. I would simply put the whole thing behind me.

I practiced my new attitude as I washed my face and brushed my teeth. It doesn't matter! I don't care! It doesn't matter! I don't care! I said to myself over and over.

I kept on saying it as I changed into my pajamas and got into bed. It doesn't matter! I don't care! And before I knew it, I'd fallen asleep.

I woke up early and lay in bed thinking about what to wear to school. What outfit could I wear to best express my new attitude?

I decided that somebody who felt the way I did (or at least the way I *wanted* to feel) would dress pretty wildly.

I decided to do a Ms. Frizzle.

Do you know who Ms. Frizzle is? She's a character in this great kids' series — the Magic School Bus books. Ms. Frizzle is a wacky teacher who takes her class on amazing class trips — like, would you believe, inside the human body!

Anyway, you must be wondering what this has to do with what I was going to wear. Well, here's the thing. Ms. Frizzle is *the wildest dresser* I have ever seen! She always wears these coordinated outfits. In *Inside the Human Body*, she wears a dress with eyes and ears and noses all over it. And her shoes have — you guessed it — tongues! In another book, she wears a dress with a caterpillar design — and on her shoes are butterflies instead of bows.

I love the way Ms. Frizzle dresses.

I decided that my theme for the day would be The Sea. I put on a blue skirt with brightly colored tropical fish printed all over it. Then I put on a green blouse. I figured that could represent seaweed or something. I pulled my hair into a ponytail, over to one side, and I pinned it with a sand-dollar barrette I made last summer.

"Claudia!" my mom called up the stairs. "You're going to be late!"

I ran to my closet and pulled out a pair of shoes. They're the plastic kind called "jellies" that I had decorated with stickers of seahorses and shells. I looked at myself in the mirror as I slid the shoes on. Was it too much? I shook my head. I looked great. I looked like someone who didn't care about what grade she got on a dumb old math test.

I ran downstairs for breakfast, and Mom gave me a big smile. "Interesting outfit, honey," she said. My parents are pretty nice about letting me dress the way I want.

I laughed and talked all through breakfast. Janine gave me a couple of strange looks. She must have thought I was a little weird, after the dejected way I'd left her room the night before. But she didn't know that this was the New, Improved Claud. The Claud who didn't care.

I had a good day at school — the best day I'd had in quite awhile. I paid attention in all my classes and even raised my hand a few times when I thought I knew the answer. My teachers seemed happy with my performance.

So did my friends.

At lunch, everybody wanted to know how I'd made the barrette and where I'd gotten the skirt. I felt pretty good. I sat with my friends and we talked about everything *but* tests, or math, or cheating.

At one point Kristy started to tell us a story about something Shawna Riverson had done during her English class that morning. Stacey shot her a Look, and Kristy stopped talking. I'm lucky to have such a sensitive best friend.

Nobody would have ever guessed that the girl in the wild outfit — the one who laughed and gossiped with her friends — cared *anything* about her grades.

By the end of the day I was exhausted. I knew I'd done a great job of convincing everybody that "it didn't matter" — but had I convinced myself? Not really. I still had this ache inside. I hated the fact that I'd been accused of cheating, and I hated the idea that there would be an F on my record where there should have been an A–.

When the last bell rang, I went to my locker and got my stuff together. I didn't have a sitting job that afternoon, so I was planning to spend some time working on a collage.

I headed out the door, deep in thought. Then, out of the corner of my eye, I saw someone go by in the opposite direction. Janine! I did a double take. Then I ran after her. "What are *you* doing here?" I asked.

"I decided it was time to do something about this awful situation," she said. "I always had a good relationship with the principal when I was at Stoneybrook Middle School. He might remember me."

Remember her! Teachers and principals never forget Janine. They'll hold her up as an example of a model student for the next fifty years.

"I know you didn't cheat, Claudia. And I'm going to talk to the principal about that test," she went on.

I couldn't believe it. All I wanted was for everybody to *forget* about the whole thing.

"I thought I told you to stay out of this!" I said to Janine angrily.

"No," said Janine solemnly, "you told Mom and Dad to stay out of it. You never said *I* couldn't help."

"But what are you going to tell him?" I asked. I didn't want the principal to know everything that had happened since the day of the test. If he did, I could be in even deeper trouble.

"Don't worry," said Janine. "I'm only going to tell him about how hard you studied, and how well you were prepared for the test. I won't say a word about the conversation you overheard in the girls' room."

"And you won't tell him about Shawna's locker, will you?" I asked.

"Claudia," said Janine, "of course I won't."

We'd been walking as we talked, and by then we'd reached the door of the principal's office. Suddenly, I felt hopeful. Janine seemed so determined. Maybe this wasn't such a bad idea anymore. I smiled at Janine and whispered into her ear. "Thanks!" I said.

She opened the door and disappeared inside. The door closed behind her.

I stood in the hallway and waited, feeling incredibly nervous. The school was pretty quiet by then, and I could hear the clock above the door ticking off the minutes. Once in a while I smiled as someone I knew walked by on his way to team practice.

The halls became completely silent. How long had Janine been in the office? I looked at the clock, but the minute hand had hardly moved. Then I heard footsteps. I looked up to see Mr. Zorzi coming down the hall.

He nodded to me when he saw me. I couldn't meet his eyes. I watched as he walked into the principal's office. What was going on in there? I was dying to know.

Just then, the door to the office opened wide. I saw the principal standing there, smiling at me. "Won't you come in, Claudia?" he asked.

I looked down at my shoes. Oh, my lord! Suddenly I felt kind of silly in my wild outfit. I'd never have worn it if I'd known I'd end up in the principal's office.

I took a deep breath and smiled back at him. Then I walked into his office. Mr. Zorzi and Janine were sitting there chatting as if they were the best of friends.

"Please sit down, Claudia," said the principal. I looked around and saw a chair next to Janine. I slipped into it. I sat up straight and folded my hands in my lap, trying to look more like a nice, normal eighth-grader and less like someone ready for a trip to the ocean floor.

Janine smiled at me, as if to say that everything was going to be all right. I gave her a weak smile in return.

"Claudia," said the principal. "Janine tells

me that you studied very hard for your math test last week."

I nodded. I didn't trust my voice.

"And she says that she's sure you knew the material," he continued.

I nodded again. Janine had always been more sure of that than I was myself!

"How did you feel when you took the test that day?" he asked.

I cleared my throat. "I — I felt good," I answered. "I felt like I had done well on the test. I felt like all that studying had been worthwhile."

Janine nodded encouragingly.

"And you are willing to sit here and tell all of us that you absolutely did not take even one little peek at anyone else's paper?" The principal looked closely at me.

"That's right," I answered in a steady voice. "I did not cheat."

"Well," said the principal, "I always think everybody deserves a chance to prove his or her innocence. Innocent until proven guilty — that's the basis of our criminal justice system, isn't it, Mr. Zorzi?"

Mr. Zorzi nodded, smiling at me.

The principal went on. "I'd like you and Janine to leave Mr. Zorzi and me alone now,"

118

he said. "We'll work out a way for you to get a fair trial. He'll let you know tomorrow what it will be." He looked at Janine, and then at me. "Is that satisfactory?"

Janine nodded and smiled. "Oh, yes. That's wonderful!" She stood up. "Thank you so much," she said.

I just sat there, stunned. Janine's plan had worked. I was going to get a chance to prove I hadn't cheated!

CHAPTER 14

I would probably still be sitting in the principal's office, in a state of total shock, if Janine hadn't grabbed my hand and dragged me home. I just couldn't believe that Janine had convinced the principal and Mr. Zorzi to give me another chance.

"Why not?" asked Janine, when I said this to her later that night. "You *deserve* a second chance."

Was this the same Janine that I'd fought with all those years? She was acting like the best big sister I could ever hope for. "So what do you think they'll decide?" I asked her. "I mean, what will I have to do to prove I didn't cheat?"

"I can't be sure," answered Janine. "But I would bet that you're going to have to convince Mr. Zorzi that you really do know that material."

"I'm nervous," I confessed.

"There's no logical reason for you to feel that way," said Janine. "But we can go over a few problems if you'd like."

I got out my math book, and we studied for about five minutes. Right away I could see that I did remember the material. In fact, it was so familiar that it was almost boring. I was ready to quit before long, and I figured that Janine was missing valuable time on her computer.

"Janine, I think I'm all set," I said. "Thanks so much for what you did today."

"That's all right, Claudia," she said. "Nobody gets away with calling my little sister a cheater."

Janine is A-OK.

I finished off my homework and then worked on my collage. It was almost done. I'd decided to give it to Janine as a thank-you present. Then I called Stacey.

"You'll never believe where I was at three-fifteen this afternoon," I said when she answered the phone. I could picture her, standing in the kitchen. If we talked for awhile she'd probably stretch the phone cord down the hall and into the coat closet. That's the only way she can get any privacy during her phone calls. I know I'm incredibly lucky to have a phone in my own room.

"Where were you?" she asked. "Not looking through Shawna's locker again, I hope!"

"No way!" I had to laugh. How could we have done that? We were lucky that we didn't get caught. I told Stacey all about the scene in the principal's office.

"Weren't you scared?" she asked.

"Are you kidding?" I answered. "I was shaking like a leaf. But it was worth it."

"What do you think they'll make you do?" she asked. I told her that it didn't matter. As long as they gave me a second chance, there was no way I was going to blow it.

We talked for awhile longer. When it was time to get off the phone, she said something that reminded me of what she'd said on that fateful night before I got my grade. "Just think, Claud. By the time we have our next meeting, this will all be over."

She was right. We had a Baby-sitters Club meeting the next afternoon. I hoped I'd have good news for everyone by then.

* * *

I wore my lucky earrings to school the next day. Even though I felt pretty confident, I figured it couldn't hurt to have a little extra good luck.

I made a point of arriving in math class a little early, so I could find out what Mr. Zorzi and the principal had decided. When I walked into his room, Mr. Zorzi was grading papers at his desk.

"Claudia," he said. "I'm glad you're here early. This is what we've decided. During class today, you're going to take the test over again."

I took a deep breath and nodded. "Okay," I said. "I'm ready."

"The test isn't exactly the same," Mr. Zorzi went on. "It covers similar material, but the questions are different." He led me to a desk at the back of the room. "The rest of the class will be studying in small groups today, so if you work with your sister tonight you won't fall behind."

I sat down at the desk and looked around me. No other desks were close by. Good! I didn't want there to be any doubt in anybody's mind that I could have cheated on *this* test.

The rest of the kids in my class were drifting

in by now. I got a couple of curious looks, but I ignored them. (I couldn't help noticing that Shawna looked like she was *dying* to know what I was up to.) I started to work on the test.

This time, I wasn't nearly as tense. Once again there were questions that looked harder and questions that looked easier; I just started with the easier ones and worked my way through the test. When I had finished, I checked my work. Then I walked up to Mr. Zorzi's desk and handed the paper to him. There was still time left in the period, so he said he'd check it right away.

I sat down at my regular desk and started to study. I wasn't exactly nervous, but I'll admit that the numbers and symbols on the page weren't making much sense to me. Once in awhile I looked up to see whether Mr. Zorzi had finished grading my test.

Just before the bell rang, Mr. Zorzi called me to his desk. I crossed my fingers as I went to the front of the room.

"You know, Claudia," said Mr. Zorzi, looking up at me as I stood in front of his desk. "I'm not just a teacher — I also help coach the boys' basketball team. And I believe that taking a test is like playing a game. You can either win the game, or you can lose it." He looked at me to see if I was following his little speech. "If you lose," he continued, "it just means you need more practice."

What was he trying to tell me? I was dying for him to get to the point.

"Good news, Claudia!" he said smiling. "You've won the game this time. You did even better on this test than on the first one. You only missed two questions."

Wow! I had aced it! All right!

"I owe you an apology, Claudia," said Mr. Zorzi. "I'm sorry that I accused you of cheating. I've learned a lesson from this."

"That's okay, Mr. Zorzi," I said. "As long as you believe me now." I was impressed that he had apologized so directly.

Then the bell rang and everybody got up to leave. "Just a minute," said Mr. Zorzi. "Shawna Riverson, please stop at my desk."

Uh-oh. I stood to one side. I figured I had a right to hear what happened next.

"Shawna," said Mr. Zorzi. "Claudia has just retaken the test she was accused of cheating on, and she has passed it with flying colors."

Shawna looked at me for a second, and then back at him. "Yeah?" she asked. "So what?"

"I believe she's demonstrated that she did not, in fact, cheat on the test," said Mr. Zorzi. "I'm going to have to ask you to prove the same thing."

Shawna turned white.

"You don't have to stay late today," he said. "You may take the test tomorrow morning during homeroom."

Wait a minute, I thought. That didn't seem fair. That would mean that Shawna would have time to study for the test. But it turned out that it didn't matter.

"I — I can't!" said Shawna. Now her face was red.

"What do you mean?" asked Mr. Zorzi. "Aren't you going to be in school tomorrow?"

"No!" said Shawna. "I mean, yes — I'm going to be in school. But I can't take the test." She rubbed her hands together anxiously.

"Shawna, what are you saying?" asked Mr. Zorzi.

"I can't take it because I don't know the material. I don't know it, and even if I studied all night I wouldn't pass the test." Shawna looked like she was about to cry. "I did it! I copied off of Claudia's paper!"

My mouth dropped open. I never expected her to actually confess.

Mr. Zorzi's mouth was open, too. Just for a moment. "Why, Shawna?" he asked. "Why did you cheat?"

She told him the story — how she'd stretched herself too thin with her activities and clubs and all. "So I just didn't think there was any other way," she finished.

"And you let me believe that Claudia was the one who had cheated?" Mr. Zorzi asked, frowning. "I think you owe her an apology."

Shawna looked at me and mumbled something I barely heard. I didn't care. I'd done it! I'd stuck this thing out and I'd proved my innocence. With Janine's help, the mystery had been solved. Now everybody would know who the real villain was. I felt like a tremendous weight had fallen from my shoulders.

Shawna, the cheater, was in tears. I almost felt sorry for her. Almost.

Mr. Zorzi sent her straight to the principal's office, and I found out later that she got suspended for two days. Plus, she got an F on that test. Poor, poor Shawna.

That's what Kristy said when I finished telling the story in the cafeteria. "Poor, poor Shawna."

"I *knew* everything would work out," said Mary Anne.

Stacey just smiled and gave me the thumbs-up sign.

I felt terrific.

CHAPTER 15

It was later that same day. I'd been in my room all afternoon, putting the finishing touches on my collage. I hummed along to the radio as I worked, and occasionally I burst into song. (I'm tone deaf, but as long as I'm sure nobody's around to hear me, I love to sing at the top of my lungs.) I was in a *great* mood.

I hadn't looked at the clock for awhile, so I was totally amazed when I checked the time. It was 5:29 — and Kristy hadn't shown up for our meeting yet. Kristy's always so punctual. I couldn't believe she wasn't already sitting in the director's chair.

I shrugged, turned up the radio, and went back to my collage. I knew everybody would start to straggle in within a few minutes.

Just as I was in the middle of belting out a really romantic love song, the door to my room flew open.

"SURPRISE!!"

I almost jumped out of my skin. What a shock! There were all my friends, plus Janine, crowded around my door. They were loaded down with bags of chips and huge bottles of Coke. Jessi was holding a platter of chocolate chip cookies. All of them were grinning at me.

I grinned back. "What's going on?" I asked.

"We wanted to do something special for you," said Mallory.

"We're proud of you," added Stacey. "You really hung in there!"

"And Kristy had the idea to make this meeting kind of a party," said Dawn. "What do you think?"

What did I think? I was overwhelmed. It's not too often that Kristy bends the rules and changes the form of a club meeting.

"I think it's terrific!" I said. "And I think you are the best friends in the world."

Then I saw Janine. She was hanging back shyly, trying to blend into the woodwork. She must have felt out of place. "And Janine is the best sister in the *universe*," I said, gesturing to her. "C'mon in, Janine. I've got something for you."

I grabbed the collage and held it behind my back for a minute. "I wanted to give you something to show you how grateful I am for all your help," I said.

"Oh, Claud," she said. "You don't have to do that! I enjoy helping you study."

"Well, even if you do, I know you have lots of other things you could use that time for," I said. "And anyway, it's not just the study help. If you hadn't talked to the principal for me, I might never have gotten a second chance on that test." I showed her the collage. "I'd like you to have this," I said.

Janine looked at it and smiled. "It's beautiful," she said. She held it up for everyone else to see. "Thank you, Claudia," she said. "I'll hang it in my room with pride."

Just then, the phone rang. I'd totally forgotten that this was our regular meeting time! Kristy took the call.

"Baby-sitters Club," she said. "Oh, hi, Mrs. Pike." She listened for a moment. "Oh, of course," she said. "I'll call you right back."

"Mrs. Pike needs a sitter for the younger kids on Saturday afternoon," said Kristy. "She said she and Mr. Pike are taking the triplets to a movie matinee, to celebrate their ungrounding."

"They're going to take them out for ice cream, afterwards," said Mallory. "I think she feels kind of bad about how long they were stuck inside. I'd watch Nicky and my sisters myself," she went on, "but Jessi and I are going to the mall on Saturday."

Mary Anne checked the record book to see who was free, and Stacey got the job. After Kristy had called Mrs. Pike back, Mal filled us in on the rest of the story about the triplets.

"You wouldn't believe how happy they are to be free again," she said. "They're acting human — it's a pleasure to be around them."

"Are they going to get their allowances back?" asked Stacey.

"Well," answered Mallory, "my parents realized that if the boys had to give up their allowances until the window was paid off, they'd be broke until they went to college!"

The Pike kids get pretty tiny allowances — I guess because there are so many of them.

"So Dad made a deal with the boys," continued Mal. "They're going to work off their debt by doing chores around the house. You know, raking leaves, cleaning out the basement — that kind of stuff."

"That's great!" said Dawn.

"Yeah, they're pretty thrilled about it," said Mal. "Now they can get back into some serious baseball-card collecting."

(The triplets don't collect baseball cards like some boys do — as investments. They just collect the cards of players they really like. That way, it doesn't cost as much — and they're just as happy.)

"That's good news, Mal," I said. "I'm glad everything's settled, for them *and* for me."

"That's right,"said Mary Anne. "We've got a lot to celebrate. By the way, did Mr. Zorzi tell you what your grade would officially be?"

I smiled. "Yes, it's true, sports fans," I said, pretending to speak into a microphone. "Claudia Kishi will go down in the record books for this one. She really earned that A–!"

"All *right*, Claud!" said Dawn.

"I'd like to propose a toast," said Kristy. Everybody scrambled to make sure they had some soda. (Dawn and Stacey were drinking plain old club soda.) Kristy held up her cup. "To Claudia," she said. "Congratulations! Nancy Drew would be proud of you. You solved the mystery, and you aced the test!"

"Yea!" yelled Jessi and Mallory together.

"Congratulations, Claud!" said Stacey.

Everybody clinked their cups together (or *pretended* to clink them; plastic doesn't clink very well) and grinned at me.

I was blushing. "Okay, you guys," I said.

"Let's get down to some serious pigging out!" I opened up the chips and passed around the cookies.

"Claudia," said Janine. "There's just one thing I want to ask you."

"Yes?" I said.

"Aren't you glad that Jessi made these cookies — instead of Gertrude?"

I laughed. Then I explained the joke to my friends, and we all broke up. That day's meeting was one of the best we've ever had.

At dinner that night, Janine told my parents what had been going on. They'd already heard that I'd gotten my A– back, but they didn't know the details. (Janine didn't tell them *everything*, for which I'm grateful.)

"Claudia, honey," said my mother. "I'm so proud of you! You really stood your ground."

"Well," I said. "I didn't want you to be disappointed in me. I knew I had to make sure my record was clear."

"Your record is *always* clear with us," said my father.

"I was worried that if I didn't do well in math you would make me quit the Baby-sitters Club," I confessed quietly.

"Oh, Claudia," said my mother. "From now

on, just make sure you let us know when you need help. Janine," she went on, "can you please give me a hand in the kitchen for a moment?"

The two of them disappeared into the kitchen, carrying our empty plates. My father jumped up from the table and went to the hall closet. When he came back, he was holding his camera.

I couldn't figure out what was going on. Then my mother and Janine reappeared. Janine was carrying a huge cake, with pink roses all over it. My dad started to snap pictures as they walked toward the table.

"What's that for?" I asked. Had I forgotten somebody's birthday?

"Look at it, Claud!" said Janine. "Read what it says!"

I looked more closely at the writing covering the cake. CONGRATULATIONS, CLAUDIA! it said. What a shock! In our family, it's usually Janine who gets the cakes and has fusses made over her — whenever she wins another prize or award. But this time, the cake was for me.

I looked around the table at the faces of my sister, my mother, and my father. They were proud of me! And, I had to admit it — I was pretty proud of myself.

About the Author

ANN M. MARTIN did *a lot* of baby-sitting when she was growing up in Princeton, New Jersey. Now her favorite baby-sitting charge is her cat, Mouse, who lives with her in her Manhattan apartment.

Ann Martin's Apple Paperbacks are *Bummer Summer, Inside Out, Stage Fright, Me and Katie (the Pest),* and all the other books in the Baby-sitters Club series.

She is a former editor of books for children, and was graduated from Smith College. She likes ice cream, the beach, and *I Love Lucy;* and she hates to cook.

Look for #41

MARY ANNE vs. LOGAN

I went into Dad and Sharon's room. I closed the door. Right away I thought, I could stop now if I wanted to. I don't *have* to call Logan.

But I called him anyway. Without even hesitating. I just picked up the receiver and punched the buttons.

Logan answered the phone. "Hi!" he said, when he heard my voice. He probably thought I was calling to apologize. He sounded as if he would accept my apology.

"Logan," I began, "this isn't going to be easy for me to say, but I'm calling — "

"To apologize, right?"

"Well, not really," I told him. "I'm calling because I think we need to cool our relationship a little. I think — "

Logan interrupted me again. "Cool our relationship? *Why?*"

"I'm going to tell you, if you'll, um, if you'll just let me talk."

"All right, all right."

"I think we've been seeing too much of each other," I said. "I feel like you're — you're overtaking my life. You plan everything for us. You always want to be with me — and I *do* like being with you — but, I don't know. I guess I feel like you don't understand me very well anymore. . . ." I trailed off.

There was a pause. Then Logan said, "Okay," in an odd-sounding voice.

"Let's try cooling things for a few weeks," I went on, my voice beginning to quiver. (I just could not believe what I was doing.) "Then when we've had some time apart, we'll pick things up again."

"Okay."

"Well . . . good-bye."

"Good-bye. Good night," said Logan.

I hung up the phone. Then I burst into tears. I cried for a long time.

Read all the books
in the Baby-sitters Club series
by Ann M. Martin